WE ARE SO CRASHING your BAR MITZVAH!!

WE INVITE YOU TO SHARE OUR JOY
WHEN OUR BELOVED SON
EBEN NOAH SIEGLER
IS CALLED TO THE TORAH
AS A BAR MITZVAH
ON SATURDAY, THE TENTH OF SEPTEMBER
TWO THOUSAND AND FIVE
AT THREE-THIRTY THE AFTERNOON

CONGREGATION BETH ISRAEL
CHAPPAQUA, NEW YORK

PLEASE JOIN US FOR A CELEBRATION
IMMEDIATELY FOLLOWING THE SERVICES

STEVE & HELEN SIEGLER

FIONA ROSENBLOOM

HYPERION PAPERBACKS · NEW YORK
AN IMPRINT OF DISNEY BOOK GROUP

If you purchased this book without a cover, you should be aware that this book is stolen property. It was reported as "unsold and destroyed" to the publisher, and neither the author nor the publisher has received any payment for this "stripped" book.

Text © 2007 by Fiona Rosenbloom and Alloy Entertainment

All rights reserved. Published by Hyperion Paperbacks for Children, an imprint of Disney Book Group. No part of this book may be reproduced or transmitted in any form or by any means, electronic or mechanical, including photocopying, recording, or by any information storage and retrieval system, without written permission from the publisher.
For information address Hyperion Books for Children,
114 Fifth Avenue, New York, New York 10011-5690.

alloyentertainment

Produced by Alloy Entertainment
151 West 26th Street
New York, NY 10001

First Hyperion Paperbacks edition, 2008
10 9 8 7 6 5 4 3 2 1
Library of Congress Cataloging-in-Publication Data on file.
ISBN 978-0-7868-3889-9
Visit www.hyperionteens.com

For Maisie, Mia, and Lili,
my three little loves

Prologue:
The Declaration of My Importance

Hi, God.

Stacy Adelaide Friedman, here.

Half inch taller, no pounds heavier, and still waiting on some other things to come in (hint, hint—nudge, nudge). But here I am, in all my underdeveloped glory, reporting for eighth-grade duty.

I'm not sure where to begin. Is my life like a Power-Point presentation up there? Can you see everything I do while I do it? Or is it like gossip, and you wait for me to fill you in? I have lots of questions for you, obviously, but first, I should probably catch you up, just in case.

God?

I have to say dank u *(that's Dutch for thank you) right off the bat because . . .*

Summer camp was spacious!

After everything that happened at my bat mitzvah, you know how worried I was to be at camp with

Lydia, much less in the same bunk.

Turns out she was worried too, and during the first campfire, while everyone else was singing "The Song That Never Ends," and wiping s'more chocolate off on their jean shorts, we told each other everything. Over graham crackers, marshmallows, and the most annoying song in the world, Lydia and I admitted how much we wanted to return to our regularly scheduled program on channel Best Friends. She promised (with a whole complex system of pinkie swears she ripped off from last year's assembly on sign language) that she would never, ever kiss a boy that I crushed. And I vowed to never uninvite her to anything ever again.

Camp was like Chap Stick; it smoothed over all the rough spots. It was a Burt's Bees kind of summer. I am proud to announce that after two months of archery, ropes courses, a musical (The Wizard of Oz), color wars, and the addition of an older, wiser, and totally cool new friend (I'm getting to her . . .), things between Lydia and me are copasetic (that's English for completely satisfactory).

So, mazel tov to you, God!

Now . . . Do you remember that cool girl from last summer? Laila Wertheimer? The ninth grader from

L.A. who got the nose job, only talked to the boy counselors, and was an extra in a movie? Well, Lydia and I totally became friends with her this year! She is SO LOL (that's a Laila phrase, God. It's IM-speak for "laugh out loud").

Laila heard that I had (see, I'm accepting the breakup—note use of past tense) a gorgeous, soccer-playing, boyfriend who lived in Italy, and also that I want (note use of present tense) to be a comedian, and thought that that was deeply cool. She also thought Lydia was the best dancer at camp, so that gave us an added leg up. We have never been friends with any older kids, so Lydia and I were both stoked. Out of all the kids at camp, Laila chose us to be friends with! And the three of us kind of ruled the summer.

Anyway, Laila taught us everything there is to know about eighth-grade style. She took us under her wing, and wised us up to the do's and don'ts. She taught us how she straightens her hair and how much eyeliner and mascara she applies (a lot), what kind of rock T-shirts work and which don't, where to thread the safety pin into the plaid skirt, and which kinds of patches are cool enough to put on our knapsacks. But get this—she slipped ten of her plastic rubber bracelets off her own wrist, and put them on us! And by the end of August, everyone at camp started dressing like her. I mean, like us.

Lydia and I ordered two Sedu ceramic hair straighteners, and after weeks of practice we can now do our entire heads ourselves, with no ridges in the back. You would hardly recognize me. And Laila got some Crest Whitestrips in a care package, and we all slept with them on every night. I can't tell if my teeth are whiter, but they FEEL whiter, and Laila said that's just as important.

What I'm getting at here, God, is that Lydia and I have transformed. We're more mature, we're trendier, we're cooler. We are going to take eighth grade by social storm, starting with a stellar debut at First Night.

As you well know, First Night is the most important night of the entire school year. Everyone in junior high meets, on the night before school starts, at the lake in the sculpture garden of PepsiCo (color me lucky for living down the road from the worldwide headquarters for Pepsi and Frito-Lay). It's not actually legal for people to be there, but no one's ever been busted. I can hardly wait for everyone's jaws to drop at our new phabulosity. Especially The Chicas'.

You might remember that last year, Kelly, Lydia, and I were practically merging with The Chicas (aka: the cool girls), Kym, Sara, and Megan. Well, this year, there is no doubt that our two groups will officially become one. I mean, if Laila Wertheimer wants to buddy up with us, then so will The Chicas. Bigger is always better, N'est-ce pas? (That's French for Is it not?)

Lydia and I are so excited to teach our second best friend, Kelly, all the new style tricks we've picked up. Except for spending the last two weeks in Florida, Kelly's been stuck at home in Rye, all by herself. She must have been bored out of her skull. I'm sure our return will be her salvation. Plus, she is SO going to love this new look.

Oh yeah, don't think I didn't notice this, but THANK YOU, GOD, for putting that thrift store smack dab in the middle of our route home from camp. Sign well sent! Lydia and I stocked up on heavily discounted retro-fab duds. We bought Kelly a shirt, too. Hers says, "Kiss me. I'm a rock star!" Ashlee Simpson, eat your synch off!

Off to Lydia's.

Don't go far.

Love,
Stacy Adelaide Friedman

P.S. How many psychiatrists does it take to change a lightbulb? Only one, but the lightbulb needs to want to really change.

1. First Night

After we pressed the powder onto our faces, Lydia and I changed our outfits fifteen times. We swapped leggings, fitted tees, plaid skirts, torn jean skirts, black spandex skirts. We piled on the bracelets: mainly more black, thin plastic ones, and tons of them.

I ended up wearing black Converse high-tops, black footless leggings, a jean skirt, a tight black T-shirt with a white peace sign spray painted on it, framed loosely at the waist by a low-slung, green studded belt. Thank God, my mother wasn't home. There was no way on earth she'd let me out of the house like this. I could hear her stodgy phrases in my head already, the slight British accent she adopted when she got angry (who'd she think she was—Madonna?).

Stacy Adelaide Friedman. I would sooner let you run naked down Interstate 95 than let you out in that getup.

Lydia was wearing a shrunken white T-shirt that said "Future Celebrity" on it (which, when we found it, we thought was a total omen), a short kilt with a big safety pin, a low-slung black belt with metal studs, and old-fashioned black mesh driving gloves she found in her attic.

Come to think of it, I could hear *her* mother's voice in my head, New York accent and all.

Lydia. Look at the calendar. Halloween isn't until October!

Lydia's face was inches from my own. "Open your mouth," she said. I did. "Pull back your lips so all your teeth are showing." Lydia planted a Crest Whitestrip along my top row, then she did my bottom. She turned to the mirror and did hers, too.

"These are half-hour ones," she said. I nodded, not wanting mine to fall out.

"I'm calling Kelly again. It's getting late, and it's like the fifteenth message I've left her since we've been home. Should I just leave the information on her machine?"

"I suppose so," I said, barely moving my mouth. I felt like a lockjawed ventriloquist. We still hadn't heard back from Kelly. How were we all going to match if we couldn't open our mouths to explain what kind of clothes we were wearing?

"When was the last time you heard from her?"

I shrugged, not wanting to talk, but then I tried a new move. I bent my head all the way back like I was watching a movie from the front row. "It's been so long, she doesn't even know about Dante yet." The edges of my Whitestrips fluttered, but ultimately stayed put.

Dante and I broke up in June, through e-mails. We both agreed that the distance between Italy and Westchester was too far, since neither set of parents would relocate. Although the breakup was mutual, I still felt bummed about it for most of the summer. He was my first boyfriend ever. I wanted Kelly to hear it from me, first.

"Weird. I don't know why she's not calling back. I've left her like a million voice mails," Lydia said before peeling off her strips.

"No clue," I said, and removed mine, too. I turned back to the full-length mirror and clamped my hair with the straightening iron. Lydia went to my desk, pressed speaker-phone, and called Kelly's cell. Predictably, we got Kelly's voice mail. Again.

"KELLY!" Lydia yelled into the phone. "Where are you?"

"WE MISS YOU!" I called from across the room.

"We need to talk First Night clothing, because we should all match. Don't you think? Call us as soon as you can. Where have you been? CALL US BACK!"

And then I yelled again from across the room, "Hey, Kelly, how does a spoiled rich girl change a lightbulb? She asks her dad for a new apartment." Lydia cracked up laughing, and hung up.

"Do you think she's mad at us?" Lydia asked me.

"I've wondered, but what could she be mad at?"

"I don't know."

"Doesn't seem logical. We haven't even talked to her. How could we have done anything?" I was secretly glad that it wasn't just my calls she wasn't returning. It's not that I wanted her to be mad at Lydia, it's that I didn't want her to be mad at just me. But still, it was weird. We hadn't talked once since we got back from camp.

"Maybe she got stuck in Florida with her grandmother or something," Lydia offered.

"Yeah, maybe," I said hopefully, even though we both knew she'd been in Florida only for the last two weeks. The likelihood of her being trapped in an airport all summer was about as high as my heels. And the heels my mother let me wear were about as high as my fingernails. AND I BITE THEM!

Lydia stood on my chair, reached up to the high shelf over my desk, and grabbed my digital camera. "Strike a pose!" she called down at me.

I turned, pouted my lips, and stuck my left hip out to

the side while managing to still hold the ceramic straightener in my hair. She jumped down and put on an old Madonna CD.

"No, you gotta look tough. We're rock chicks, not supermodels."

I pulled my hip in, unpouted my lips, stared dead into the camera, affectless, annoyed, even.

FLASH.

"Perfect," Lydia said, turning the camera around so I could see the display screen.

"I love this song!" Lydia said and turned up the volume on my stereo. There was pounding from the other side of the room. And then my little brother's strained, high, unbroken voice,

"TURN THAT DOWN! PEOPLE ARE CONDUCTING SCIENCE EXPERIMENTS IN HERE!" Arthur screamed from his bedroom.

I turned the volume knob down—slightly—and while Lydia continued to dance, I picked up the camera.

"Vamp it up, rock star," I said.

Lydia spun and then did the choreographed dance from the old "Vogue" video. She crossed her arms over one another, put her hands up to the side of her face, and spun them round and over her head. She was an exceptionally good dancer. Even when she was mock dancing, she had talent. "That's how we should walk in to First Night," she said.

"Like we're having a seizure?" I asked, sarcastically.

"That is SO not LOL. No. Like, we're onstage. I mean, maybe that's being immodest, but First Night is all about who got cool and who got hot over the summer, and who didn't, right?"

"Right," I said.

"Well," she said somewhat sheepishly. "Don't you think we sort of got cool?"

I stared at myself in the full-length mirror that hung lopsided on the back of my bathroom door. Although I had yet to apply my smoky eyes and upper lip mole, I still felt very grown up, like a girl going into junior high should. This was so unlike last year, when my mother still chose my clothes for me.

I turned back to her and held the camera up to her face. Her eyes squinched shut and her mouth dropped open, like she was screaming into a microphone.

FLASH.

"Yeah. I guess you're right. We did get a little bit hot," I said.

She walked over to me, took the camera, and got a picture of us both. "Evidence!" Lydia said, flipping it around.

It was exciting. We looked good. But someone was still missing.

"Let's try Kelly again," I said.

Lydia walked over to the phone, but something seemed to strike her and she turned to face me, pale.

"What?" I asked.

"Maybe she gained more weight. Remember last summer, she was embarrassed about going swimming because she didn't want anyone to see her in a bathing suit?" Lydia said.

I felt instantly mortified. Kelly always had a bit of a weight problem. Nothing too drastic—just an extra layer of baby fat that was really stubborn. We all called it her black belt, because it fought back when she was trying to diet.

"Yeah. And we've been so braggy about our new look. I've told her at least four times through e-mail and now we've left a million messages on her voice mail. She must feel really bad."

The last thing I wanted was for Kelly to feel left out when she saw us at First Night in our new look. We had to make a conscious effort to make Kelly feel included.

"Let's act really normal if she has gained weight. Like we don't even notice it," I said.

"Good plan."

STACY FRIEDMAN'S STATEMENT OF FACT: Sometimes after excluding people (i.e. my best friend, Lydia, from my bat mitzvah), you become extra conscious of including people.

Lydia and I bared our teeth to each other. After a whole summer of Whitestrips, they could have doubled for tiles in a Mr. Clean commercial, they were so white. I finished straightening the other side of my hair. There was a sizzling sound because I hadn't waited for my hair to fully dry. The smell of burned hair floated under my nose. Gross.

"Hey, maybe we should call The Chicas and meet them earlier? That way we can all walk in together, so there's no mistaking that we're one group."

"THE group," Lydia said. "I'll call them while you go in your mother's bathroom and collect all her new makeup."

"Done."

I walked down the hall to my mother's overly floral bedroom, feeling more confident than ever. First Night determined your social standing for the rest of the year. And Lydia and I were going to First Night completely transformed. Even Kym, the head Chica, would be impressed with us. And I don't think she was ever impressed with anyone.

I returned with the makeup, and dumped it on top of my bright pink-and-white gingham bedspread.

"Did you talk to Megan or Sara?" I asked.

"Messages," Lydia answered.

"What about Kym? Did you call Kym?"

"Message."

I glanced up (I had one of those cool clocks that projected the time on the ceiling.) There wasn't a lot of time left before we had to go, and we still hadn't heard back from Kelly. Lydia ran over to the CD player and replayed track number seven ("Don't Tell Me"—Madonna), our "getting dressed track," blasting to maximum volume.

Arthur banged on the wall and shouted, "SOME OF THE PEOPLE WHO LIVE HERE ARE SCIENTISTS!"

Lydia and I stood together, side by side, in front of the mirror. I handed her a black eyeliner pencil and kept one for myself, and then, in unison, we leaned forward and started to outline our eyes, like Laila had taught us. Then we stood back and examined ourselves.

"Spacious," Lydia said, using one of our invented lingo terms.

"Totally spacious," I agreed.

"SOME OF US APPRECIATE A RESPITE FROM THE CACOPHONY SO WE CAN FOCUS OUR ENERGIES ON PATENTS AND INVENTIONS!"

We put Kelly's rock star shirt in a plastic bag. And then we hooked arms, walked out of my bedroom, down the hall, and out into the world toward First Night. First everything.

2. The Exaggetorium

We biked down Lincoln Avenue to PepsiCo. When we got there, the velvet rope was draped across the entrance, its message clearly saying CLOSED.

Lydia and I looked at each other. We had never broken the law before. Was this even considered breaking the law? After all, the eighth, ninth, and tenth graders had been doing this for years. First Night was a tradition, so it wasn't like we were the only people sneaking into the sculpture garden to hang out by the lake.

We got off our bikes and rolled them under the velvet rope while we ducked under alongside them. We hopped back on and pedaled fast toward the lake. Every few feet I looked back to see if security guards were running after us with billy clubs and handguns. But the path behind us was clearer than skin on Proactiv.

We saw tons of kids as we neared the lake. And everyone

looked tan. Not even fake tan, but summer tan, camp tan, family vacation tan. And in order to make their tans stand out they wore bright clothing. That old trick.

Thankfully, no one looked as fashion forward as we did. We were rebelliously pale. "Good luck with the street miming!" Arthur had called after us when we left the house. What did he know? He was so clueless he couldn't have picked style out of *Vogue*.

We got off our bikes and looked around to see where everyone else had tossed theirs. But there were none in sight. I looked at Lydia.

"Where are all the bikes?" I asked.

"Beats me," she answered.

"Are people not riding their bikes anymore?" I wondered, totally worried this was a major faux pas.

"I don't know," she said, equally worried. We quickly tossed our bikes down in the grass and walked away from them as fast as we could, as if they didn't belong to us.

As we walked through the crowd, I began to feel very self-conscious. I had been so worried about impressing The Chicas with the new look, I forgot that there were other people in our school. Older kids. And they were intimidating, all in their own little groups.

There was a cluster of earthy, granola types in their Birkenstocks, wearing their homemade patchouli-scented essential oils. There were the artists in their paint-splattered clothes; the jocks who, for lack of imagination, wore baseball and basketball shirts. The older kids dressed in a variety of ways: designer, thrift, prepster, hipster, vagabond, street. But no one, not one person, looked like us. Instead of standing out the way we wanted, we blended in, because everyone, and I do mean EVERYONE, was trying some new look to set themselves apart, too.

A few steps later, we saw The Boys: Rob Mancuso and Andy Goldfarb. They looked pretty much exactly the same (read: basic) but taller. I hoped that Andy thought I looked hot, and regretted that he hadn't loved me back last year when I had loved him so much. Well, at least before I loved Dante.

"Don't look too closely," Lydia whispered, "but Andy Goldfarb got zitty."

I smiled.

We scanned the crowd for Kelly, but there was no sign of her. I was really beginning to worry about her weight. What if she was so ashamed she didn't even show up for First Night?

"I don't see anyone," Lydia said. "Maybe we came too early?"

A bunch of ninth and tenth graders in skimpy outfits (so flimsy they could have been made from cheesecloth) were sitting on the bench next to these plaster-cast people sculptures that sat there permanently. They were joking around; one kid was pretending to make out with one of the figures, another was curled up in the lap of another. They were laughing, having a great time; all eyes were on them. They were the kings and queens of First Night, maybe even the whole school, and they knew it.

We were the newbies. We would be joining them, entering a new building we weren't used to, entering into their way of life, onto their premises. We would be sharing hallways with them, the cafeteria, the bathrooms, the school yard. Our old building, the K–7 building, would be sitting across campus, outgrown by us and small and provincial in comparison. My palms began to get clammy.

"The Chicas aren't even here yet," I added, pointing out the obvious.

Marni Gross walked by the upperclassmen, trying hard in last year's clothes, the famed terry cloth halter-top dress worn over jeans. She was such a Don't. The older kids whispered and outright snickered when she passed.

Poor Marni, she was hopeless. She had the personality of

an OfficeMax catalog. She kept walking back and forth, checking her cell phone, rotating her head, left to right, pretending to look for someone. But she had no group. She was fake looking for fake-late people.

I was so glad I wasn't in her place. *Thank you, God, for not putting me in Marni Gross's shoes.* I loved having the security of a group. There was no better feeling in the world.

"Is there lipstick on my teeth?" I displayed my Antarctic caps, the white continent living inside my mouth.

"All clear."

"Is my mascara clumping?"

Lydia inspected. "Lashes are as separated as your parents."

I tapped my feet. I snapped my fingers. Where the hell was Kelly? Where were The Chicas? I felt out of sorts and kind of awkward with all this makeup on, in this tight black ensemble. Were we supposed to just stand here alone, just the two of us, while everyone else began to form clusters? Where was our group? I started twirling my hair. I felt a warm hand over mine. Lydia held it.

"Stop fidgeting. You're acting like Julia Roberts in *Pretty Woman* when she doesn't know which fancy fork to use."

She was right. I was nervous and I was letting it show. I had to pretend I was on the red carpet: poised, self-possessed, wearing a three-million-dollar Bulgari necklace, best friends with Scarlett Johansson and recently engaged to Jake Gyllenhaal.

Lydia pulled out her new cell phone and checked for messages. I looked over her shoulder enviously. My cell phone was so big and clunky, it looked like a VCR. No phone messages. I pulled out Oral-B teeth-whitening gum and stuck about four pieces into my mouth. Lydia followed suit.

When the ninth graders left the bench to climb on the Henry Moore sculpture, Lydia grabbed my hand and we made a beeline for the prime seats. The ninth graders turned as they were leaving and gave us the up and down—they scanned our bodies from toe to head, like we had bar codes on us.

This whole judging thing, it wasn't for me. It made my stomach hurt. I feared that at any minute someone was going to hold up a scorecard with a number on it.

"Oh, my God," Lydia said, her voice shocked into a different octave. I reflexively clutched her arm.

"What?"

She pointed to a beautiful, thin, blond-haired girl, who was walking right toward us.

"It's Kelly," she said, in disbelief.

Sure enough, walking our way, with a huge smile, and an expression that I can recall only as glowy, Kelly Mooreland walked toward us. She looked A-M-A-Z-I-N-G. She hadn't gained weight at all! She was tan and toned, her arms like a sinewy dancer's. Her braces were off, her teeth were straight, white, and sparkling. Her thick, long, hair hung in soft waves and bore the most fabulous towheaded streaks. She looked au naturel, like a mermaid. She was way taller than we were. Kelly was . . . well, hot.

Lydia and I just sat there on the bench, stunned, jaws dropped.

"You guys!" Kelly squealed. "I've missed you!" She ran the last couple of feet and enveloped us in huge hugs.

"Kelly. Wow," was all I could manage.

"I know, right? It's crazy," she said, like she couldn't quite believe it herself. "But look at *you* guys," she said, running her finger down the row of Laila Wertheimer's plastic bracelets on my wrist. "So this was the look you were talking about! So awesome!"

"You look great, Kel," Lydia said.

"So good," I agreed.

Kelly's smile was wider than the red velvet rope at PepsiCo's entrance. Even though her body was harder, her appearance was softer. She had on a sheer turquoise Victorian ruffle top, with a tank trimmed with lace peeking out from underneath.

She was also wearing brown gauchos and black flats. She looked good; she just didn't look like us.

"Crest Whitestrips?" I asked, pointing to her shimmering smile.

"Nope, when they took my braces off, they couldn't believe how white they were. It was as if the braces had protected my enamel or something."

"Did Bianca do your fabulous streaks? They look so natural," Lydia wanted to know, pulling at her own mousy brown hair. "I'm so overdue."

"It's all sun, sister. All sun. I spent practically every day at the beach."

"Did your mom finally let you get a gym membership? You're so buff!" I wondered.

"I wish, but no. The baby fat just sort of melted off. I swear, I grew like four inches and my chub magically disappeared! My black belt didn't even put up a fight!"

We couldn't believe it. Here she was, without any effort whatsoever, a total goddess.

I was so jealous, but in a good way. I had a Why-didn't-that-happen-to-me? twinge. I thought that Lydia and I had transformed, but it was Kelly who was the real before and after. We had just changed our clothes, whereas Kelly had become beautiful. And I was happy for her. I was. Really.

I hugged her again, and over her shoulder I spotted The Chicas coming up the hill and toward us. Kym Armstrong—head Chica—was leading Megan Riley and Sara Langley. The broad smile on Kym's face was aimed directly at us. I was relieved to know that we had a definite group, and a permanent place at the lunch table. I smiled big, almost laughed, and dropped my arms from Kelly in preparation for Kym's overly affectionate hug.

Kym looked just the same: tall, blonde, upturned nose. Even her attitude was the same: instead of an aura, Kym had a slightly snooty air surrounding her. Soon I noticed that all of them, Megan, Sara, and Kym, were dressed the same as Kelly. They were in sheer lace tops and gauchos. Even Megan, who was very fashionista (last year she wore shower rings as bracelets and dyed the front of her hair bright pink), was now wearing her hair long and wavy.

Kym was so close, she was almost at Kelly's back; and as soon as she was in touching distance, I reached up my arms to embrace her. Only she reached her arms out and lobster-clawed Kelly on both sides of her thin waist instead. Kelly screamed, startled, then turned around and laughed. Kym gave Kelly a long and warm hug, while my arms sort of froze in this awkward half-raised position. I dropped them, embarrassed that I had been caught looking so enthusiastic.

"Ladies," Kym said to me and Lydia.

"Hi, Kym," I said, going in—and reciprocally now—for the hug. It was halfhearted, stiff, and cursory, like the kind you give to an aunt. How dare she obligatory-hug me!

Everyone finished saying their hellos and then started fawning over one another's outfits.

"Going on tour?" Kym asked, slightly jokey, slightly mean-spirited. Lydia and I looked down at our outfits. I suddenly felt like an idiot. Here we were with our dumb smudged raccoon-eyes and plastic black bracelets, and there they were in these soft, feminine glamorous outfits. She was right. We stood out like Courtney Love at a Sarah McLachlan concert.

"Ohmygod, this?" I said, looking at my outfit and motioning to Lydia's. "No, it's a total joke. We thought it was LOL, you know like . . . what Marni Gross would look like if she got beat up by Fiona Apple," I said trying to act as convincing as I could.

"Yeah. We thought it'd be funny," Lydia repeated.

Kym looked unconvinced. But it was Megan who saved the day.

"Hey, guys, look at this," she said as she lifted her hair, exposing her ear. We all gasped. Her mother had let her get two more holes. She had four earrings in her left ear now. She was so cool.

"I've discovered my inner Gwyneth," Sara announced.

Lydia and I were confused.

"Yoga. I'm dedicating my life to yoga," she said as she held her hands together under her chin in a prayerlike position.

"You know how to do yoga?" I asked.

Sara flushed. "Well, no. Not yet. But I really like the idea of it. Thinking about it just calms me."

"Come on, girls, holler!" Kym said as she floated past us and grabbed a seat on the bench. She draped a leg over the sculpture, and gave a sexy pose, which everyone laughed at a little too hard.

Then Kym took off her bag, and Sara rifled through its contents, pulling out a Mason Pearson, and began brushing Kym's hair. Lydia and I stood in front of Kelly and The Chicas, arms at our sides, trying not to seem awkward. How was it that they were all dressed alike? Was it just a coincidence? Kelly got up from the bench and grabbed my hands.

"So, tell me everything! How was camp?" Kelly asked.

Kym leaned into our space from the bench and interrupted before we could answer.

"Pause. Kelly, ohmygod, I forgot to tell you. This morning,

at Starbucks we saw Derek! Remember Derek? Atomic Wings and Mustard Jugs? And what was the name of our band again?" Kelly turned to Megan, but before Megan could answer, Kelly yelled, "Bad Breath and the Monotones!" and started convulsing with laughter.

What was this? They'd started a band? I didn't even know Kelly could play an instrument.

"Doo doo da-da, a dum dum!" all the girls sang together, and then fell apart laughing again. Lydia and I looked at each other. Uh-oh. I suddenly felt very outer circle. There was some sort of balance shift, one that included private jokes, codes, memories, and feminine, flowy clothes.

"You started a band?" I asked.

"Oh, not a real one, just, oh it's too complicated. So tell me . . . camp?"

I forced a smile. "It was great, we made friends with this girl Laila who was totally incredible and knew everything possible about fashion and—"

Megan interrupted, shrieking, "And 'Would they notice?' Remember that? 'Do you think they'd even notice if she had her baby right now?'" she said, imitating some other voice, a guy voice. This Derek guy, probably. Sara was shaking, her shoulders were rising and falling with more action than the lines on a polygraph test, a tear fell from her eye. And Kelly almost dropped to the grass with laughter.

I felt an urgent need to level the playing field, or at least to shift the attention away from all this talk of them hanging out. After they calmed down a bit, Kelly asked, "How's Dante?"

"Oh . . . uh . . ." I stammered. The girls looked at me, anxious to hear and perhaps, maybe even a little envious? "He wanted everyone to know he says hi. Or rather, *ciao*. Oh, and Kelly, I don't know who this Derek guy is, but you might want to forget all about him, because Dante says he has an Italian boyfriend for you."

"Really?"

"Yeah. His name is Antonio," I lied. "He's moving to Westchester in a couple of months. He's so LOL." Oh, jeez. What was I going to do in a few months? Hold a casting session for Italian boys?

"Really? To Westchester? Is he cute?"

"I'll know soon because we're planning a family trip to sail around Italy on Dante's family's yacht. Apparently he's like, really rich."

"Pause. Dante is rich?" Kym asked, suddenly interested in what I had to say. "He doesn't dress rich."

"Well, you know what they say—don't judge a book by

its movie! But seriously, he's filthy rich. He's been sending me like tons of presents all summer. He's like, ohmygod. Seriously, you guys, he's like the best boyfriend ever."

I could feel Lydia's eyes boring into my skull. Okay, exboyfriend, I thought. A minor, two-letter technicality.

STACY FRIEDMAN'S THOUGHTS ON LYING: Sometimes lying is for the good of the people. And sometimes when you lie you're doing it to inflate your self-importance, and therefore your social standing. I was doing both. I was dual lying.

"Well, what'd he send you?" Sara asked.

I couldn't bear to look at Lydia, but I was just hoping that her expression was not giving me away. I don't know why I was saying these things, but I didn't know any other way to break into their circle of secrets and shared moments. I craved whatever it was they had with Kelly. I wanted it too.

"God, I can't remember, just like, stuff. Like jewelry and perfume and like, so much Italian stuff. He sent me this food basket with ricotta, olives, insalata Caprese, pastrami—" I was definitely going off the deep end here, I mean, food? Whose boyfriend sends them food?

"That is so sweet, he's like sending you all these Italian foods," Sara gushed. "I have got to get myself a boyfriend. You are so lucky, Stacy."

"Yeah, you really are," Kym agreed.

"Totally jealous," Megan added.

They were jealous of me! This was working.

Suddenly, kids started murmuring loudly about something. People's heads were turning from the lake, toward the single car lane that headed toward the lake.

"Hey, Lydia, let me borrow your camera for a second," Kym bossed. Lydia lifted the camera off her neck and handed it to her.

Out of nowhere, an enormous white Hummer limousine appeared and pulled to a slow stop in front of the lake. Kym yelled, "Come on, Chicas! He's here! He's here!"

Who's here?

Kelly grabbed my hand and said, "Come on, you guys! You won't believe it. This is going to be the best thing ever!" Lydia grabbed my hand and we all ran to meet the limousine, each eighth grader vying for a prime spot.

How did everyone seem to know what was about to happen? Lydia and I glanced at each other. It was like, suddenly, at every turn, Kelly knew something that Lydia and I didn't. How many times had she and The Chicas hung out this summer? Did she spend all her time with them, or just some? Maybe it was just one time, but it was like an entire day. That would be okay. Maybe.

Somehow The Chicas all managed to find a space in the front. Lydia, Kelly, and I were separated from them by four people, but we were in the front row as well. I couldn't even imagine who might be in the car. Oprah? Seriously, I just had no idea.

3. The VIPs (or The Very [Un] Important Plebeians)

A chauffeur, dressed in a double-breasted tuxedo, got out of the limousine, walked around to the other side, and opened the back door. A boy with the straightest and blondest hair I've ever seen stepped out of the limo. He had an upturned nose, and his cheeks were patched with red, like he had just stepped inside from a winter storm. He was around our age and dressed in an oversize white tuxedo and top hat. The tuxedo jacket was long, making him look more like a doctor than Usher, which was the look he was clearly going for. And pinned to his lapel was a gold letter E.

He was holding a silver tray, and on top of the tray were small, red velvet coin purses. A second or two after he exited the limousine, another boy emerged. He was also wearing an oversize white tuxedo, with a gold letter E; he kept shrugging and flexing his back in order to keep the suit from slipping off his shoulders. Finally, he unbuttoned the coat and took it off, folding it over his arm like a waiter about to pour wine.

The blond boy turned and motioned for the second boy to put the jacket back on, which he did, immediately. I could not stop staring at him.

FLASH. Kym took a picture.

"EBEN! We love you!" Megan Riley called as she jumped up and down, jockeying for the blond boy's attention. All The Chicas started jumping up and down.

The Boys from our school seemed nonchalant and watched from the background. I saw Andy Goldfarb roll his eyes at Eben, so I guessed they weren't friends. Who the hell was Eben?

Eben snapped his fingers at Kym and said, "Hey there, cousin. You look better than ever, baby. Better. Than. Ever!"

Lydia and I looked at each other. We didn't even know Kym had family. She seemed so worldly and independent; she seemed to come without parents. And why were they all fainting over this Eben person? He wasn't even so cute, and he was talking like a used-car salesman.

Now, the other boy . . . the other boy was something else. He had honey-brown curly hair, but the loose kind of curls, like macaroni, and it was overgrown, shaggy. He seemed kind of shy, and when he looked up, I saw that he had freckles across the bridge of his nose, a slight smattering on his cheeks. Just like me!

"Hey, Oliver, shut the limo door. The air conditioner's on, man!"

Oliver.

Oliver shut the limousine door and then stood off to the side, like he had been roped into whatever this was they were doing. I guess his E pin designated him as Eben's helper. I bet he'd rather be running in some wide-open grassy field, blowing dandelion fluff into the air, professing his everlasting love TO ME! I had the butterflies. He was dreamy.

Eben opened up one of the coin purses and pulled out a necklace with a gold letter E pendant that matched his lapel pin exactly. He swung it back and forth like he was trying to hypnotize the crowd. Oliver paced near the three of us, and I tried not to stare, but it was very difficult. You try being in arm's reach of the planet perfection and see how you do. Eben looked at the crowd in an overly confident, almost smarmy way. An eighth grader behind me whispered to her friend, "If you get a necklace it means you're invited to his bar mitzvah."

I turned to Lydia and Kelly. They were fear-struck. We all were, and I wanted to lessen the intensity of this moment, so I anxiously did what any normal comic-in-training would do: I made jokes.

"What's with the white tuxes? Are they Ice Capades escapees?"

Oliver lifted his head and looked over at me. I was afraid he might have been mad, but he was all smiles. He walked over to us, leaned into me, and whispered conspiratorially, "Actually, we've just come from a butler and waiter–off. We were voted out early. During appetizers."

I looked up at him, awed. Was this what they meant by soul mate?

"That's funny!" I said.

"Funny ha-ha, or funny strange?"

"Does it really matter? As long as the word funny is in there, I'd take funny looking."

"I'd take funny smelling," he said.

We looked at each other, slightly amazed at this insta-connection, but then all eyes were back on Eben as the crowd suddenly *oohed* when he held up the silver tray again—as if he were a game show host tempting the contestants with potential winnings.

I turned back to Oliver. "Just so you know, I used to be a lot taller, but I entered a height-off and got cut in the first round."

"Did you just make that up?" he asked, surprised.

"Yup. I suffer from an advanced case of clever."

"You're better off than me. I just got my X-rays back, and unfortunately, it looks as though I've lost all my common sense. I'm having an operation soon. It's only logical."

I could have done this all day. But Eben shot Oliver a look of annoyance.

"The boss is glaring," Oliver said, and walked back to Eben. Eben handed Oliver the silver tray, and Eben led the way to Kym. He stood in front of her and Oliver lowered the tray while Eben picked up a necklace. Her face expressed entitlement, like she was better than everyone else for getting the first necklace. Umm, hello? She was his cousin, for crying out loud. Nevertheless, Kym pressed the E necklace to her chest, then scanned the crowd with a long, slow look and a smirk that, if translated into letters, would have spelled out: L-O-S-E-R-S.

Eben walked over to Megan and Sara, and Oliver trailed him with the tray. I started getting excited. Megan and Sara squeezed hands, and each accepted a necklace. Kym took their picture. FLASH. One after the other. FLASH.

I had never been to a bar mitzvah where the invitations were handed out like this: from two boys from another school in a limousine and tuxedos. The whole town had apparently been talking about it all summer. To be invited to something I didn't even know about was exciting enough, but to be chosen like this, in front of a crowd of all my friends and ninth graders I didn't even know, was as life changing as getting plucked out from behind the counter of your Wok 'n Roll job at the food court to star in a Hollywood movie.

Megan and Sara shrieked at the delicate E that hung at the end of their slinky gold links. "Thank you, Eben," they yelled in unison, slinging the chains over their heads and grinning at each other like they'd just gotten off their braces.

I squeezed Lydia's hand as Eben eyed the rest of the crowd. Oliver stood behind him, smiling in our direction. We were all restless and clamoring without making a sound or moving much. We must have looked like penguins, all up on our toes, chests out and proud, vying for Eben's gaze. Was this what it was like to try to get into a nightclub?

Eben surveyed the scene, his eyes sweeping in our direction. I'd need a new dress to wear to the party. Something to catch Oliver's attention. Sure, I was funny, but I wanted him to also think I was hot. Maybe I'd forgo the rocker look and dress more like Kelly and The Chicas—with my hair up, but loose, like early Renaissance. Maybe I'd put flowers in my hair, like a fairy, or wood nymph. I could even match my shoes and my purse with them. I could barely contain my excitement.

Eben and Oliver walked over to Lydia and me and stood staring at us for a minute. Eben inspected us like we were suspicious moles growing on someone's hairy back. Oliver was smiling and seemed excited for me to be getting a necklace. And then a horrible thought shot across my mind like lightning.

What if Eben invited me but not Lydia or Kelly? Should I still accept the invitation?

I really hoped that we'd all get one. But everyone knows that it's impolite to turn down an invitation handed to you. So, of course they'd understand. I'd make sure they knew it was nothing personal.

I could feel the sweat drip as Lydia and I clutched at each other. Eben shifted his eyes from us to Kym, as if asking her what to do. Kym didn't say anything. She just stood stony-faced and shook her head, ever so slightly, side to side. No.

My face turned red from the proverbial smack. And then the wind left me, as if all the air had been shocked out of my system. NO? Eben slowly backed away and Oliver looked confused. Eben walked a few paces until he was standing in front of Kelly. He turned to Kym once more and this time, Kym smiled. Eben motioned with his head to Oliver, and Oliver reluctantly walked away from me with the silver tray and lowered it in front of Eben. Eben reached for the necklace.

My mouth dropped open. Had we just been dissed? We were being passed over in favor of Kelly? I desperately tried to make eye contact with Oliver, but he wasn't turning around. It was like he was purposefully NOT looking in my direction. Kelly, with the necklace dangling in front of her face, looked over at us, unsure of what to do.

"Take the necklace!" Kym egged from the side.

"Yeah, take it," Sara said.

"YAY. We can all go together!" Megan clapped and shouted. That burned.

Kelly turned back to Eben and very slowly reached her hand out to take the necklace.

FLASH.

She slipped it over her head and then turned to us, making a caught-in-the-middle "eek" face. Eben waved and then shouted, "See you at the Oscars!" and slipped back inside the limousine as if he had already won the award. Oliver took the tray with the remaining necklaces and ducked back inside the limousine. He didn't say good-bye or wink or anything. He didn't even look at me. But the car sped out of sight and the crowd quickly dispersed.

Some girls I didn't know clamored over to The Chicas to get a look at the necklaces. Others skulked away, but Lydia and I remained frozen, still clutching hands, our necks with cricks in them from being turned for so long in Kym and Kelly's direction. We were dumbfounded—literally, struck dumb. Kelly was fondling the gold pendant, and our mouths were hanging open, all the way down to the center of Earth.

4. Sloppy Joes and Sloppy Seconds

Everything was very confusing inside Jefferson Junior High. The gaucho pants I'd bought from the local Mandee the night before were very itchy, and the lace on my pale pink Victorian shirt was irritating my skin. My straight hair kept falling into my eyes so that I could barely see where I was supposed to go. On top of that, I'd have to tell my mom to add me to the school bus list from now on, because since no one was riding their bikes anymore, I had to walk to school. And it was brutal. We're talking many miles, people.

The floors in our junior high were marked by letters and the classrooms by number. My schedule looked like some sort of bingo card. West Civ 2F, Geo A6, Span B7. I was trying to figure out where homeroom was, and was pushed and shoved out of the way as the first bell rang. The upperclassmen were loud; they yelled, chewed gum, played music, and play-slapped each other. They looked so mature, while I just looked my age. Maybe even younger than thirteen.

I passed a row of lockers and headed in the general direction of homeroom (B4). From down the hall I could see that one locker was decorated in shiny gold paper. I smiled and hoped that one day, someone would decorate my locker in shiny gold paper. I leaned in to read it, and saw that the gold paper was decorated with the words CONGRATULATIONS, CHICA! LOVE, THE CHICAS. Printouts of the pictures that Kym had taken at First Night were glue-sticked up and down the length of the locker. The signatures on the bottom read, *Megan* and *Sara*. My stomach sank, and I hoped that it was Kym's locker. Not Kelly's.

Homeroom was abuzz. I scanned the room, recognizing only a quarter of the faces. Even the classroom felt more mature. There wasn't corkboard with colorful rules or reminders tacked up. Just the basics: a blackboard, a map, a putty-colored teacher's desk, and right-handed plastic chair-desks for the students. Andy Goldfarb was scratching his name into the laminated desktop with the edge of a paper clip. The Chicas huddled in the far corner. All the seats around them were taken. I tried to make eye contact with them to wave or something, but they were too involved in their own little plan-making; it seemed impossible to penetrate their minicoven. Their E necklaces were swinging from the chains around their necks. I sat in an open seat near the teacher's desk and waited for my name to be called. Just as the teacher got to me, Lydia and Kelly ran in and plopped down in vacant seats next to me. Thank God!

"Is this place confusing or what?" Lydia asked, catching her breath.

I noticed that Lydia had abandoned the rocker look right alongside me.

"Tell me about it! It took me an hour to find this room," Kelly said.

I was glad to see that Kelly was necklace free. I wanted to say something about the bar mitzvah, so that it'd be out in the open and the three of us wouldn't have to pretend that there was nothing unusual going on, but I couldn't find the words. I dreaded confrontation more than I dreaded throwing up.

I heard this whistle sound, and Kelly's head snapped to attention with the same suddenness and elasticity that Arthur's had back when he was overweight and smelled brownies. Kym was waving her over, although there was nowhere for Kelly to sit. And Kelly was already sitting and comfortable, thank you very much, with her friends. No, pardon me, with her BEST FRIENDS. Kelly mouthed something back and stayed put.

STACY FRIEDMAN'S ADMITTANCE OF SOME SUDDEN AND

UNPLEASANT EMOTIONS SHE IS CURRENTLY EXPERIENCING: I do not like to feel left out. AT ALL. It is a most unpreferable experience, and the emotion that accompanies it is, acutely and distinctly, mad nasty.

Homeroom came and went without further incident. After gym class, Lydia and I ducked into the upstairs girls' bathroom for damage control. Rope-climbing made us sweat, and sweat made us frizzy. Math and biology were uneventful. But then there was lunch.

Lunch was sloppy joes, my absolute favorite. Lydia's favorite was tacos, but she loved sloppy joes also, as they were kindred beef recipes. But that was the only thing about my first junior high lunch that was familiar.

The cafeteria was busier than any cafeteria I had ever been in before. In our old building we once ruled the roost, but now, in this building, we *were* the roost. These high school girls didn't just wear makeup; they wore an entire MAC makeup counter. They were noisy and called too much attention to themselves and wore, like, designer clothes and went into New York City to shop and tried to get into Marquee and Bungalow 8. I bet they even had fake IDs! And now, here they were, in a cafeteria we were all going to share, eating sloppy joes side by side. It was nerve-wracking.

Lydia and I stood with our trays, scanning for empty spots. The room was bumper to bumper with long, white, picnic-style tables. I had never seen so many strangers in one place. We wanted to save enough room for Kelly and The Chicas, but everything looked taken, and we felt too self-conscious to wander aimlessly through the aisles. It'd be like asking for it—a bear tapping a hunter on the shoulder. Then I saw a lone arm waving back and forth. Kelly!

We walked over and the other kids with her came into view: Megan, Sara, and, of course, Kym. Kelly pulled over a free chair she had been saving and then scooted over to make room for us.

That small niggling feeling of being excluded washed over me again. Did they all meet after class and come to the cafeteria together? Why hadn't they waited for us?

Kym was holding court. "Ladies," she said as Lydia and I sat, waving her hands to call attention to herself, as if what she was going to say was the most electrifying thing ever.

But let me tell you, it was not. It was downright depressing.

"Ladies, this party is going to be ill. Like so sick that MTV is considering doing a reality show on it. This will be better than the actual Oscars. I know, too, because my cousin's friend's father went once. He was b-o-r-e-d. Pause, amendment, he was comatose. But this party is gonna be off the chain." She took a deep breath and glanced in our direction. "Sorry to be talking about it in front of you guys, but like, you understand. Eben is my cousin, after all. Holler," Kym finished.

"We don't need to talk about all this right now, anyway," Kelly muttered.

"Oh, my God, Kelly, I totally know what you should wear!" Kym suddenly screeched.

"What?" Kelly asked.

"That gold crochet headband in your closet."

Hold up. Kym had been in Kelly's closet?

"Yeah, maybe. I can figure it out later," Kelly said quickly.

Everyone sort of quieted, getting it, for a minute, that we weren't ALL invited to the best party in the entire hemisphere.

Kym turned to us and, using her best fake-nice voice, said, "We'll tell you guys all about it. We swear."

"Sounds like it's really going to be a great bar mitzvah. It's gonna be LOL," I said.

"It would be better if you both were there," Kelly said, looking down at her full plate of untouched sloppy joe.

"Well, I'll probably be in Italy then, anyway," I said.

"Oh, you and your family are really going to go?" Kelly asked.

"And Lydia," I added without looking at Lydia.

"You're going, too?" Kelly asked, with what I sensed was a hint of jealousy.

Uh-oh. I didn't want to hurt Kelly's feelings. It wasn't her fault we weren't invited to Eben's bar mitzvah and she was. It wasn't her fault that Kym being in her closet unleashed something else in me, another wave of jealousy that I could not seem to quell.

"We have an extra ticket. You can come, too," Lydia said.

I was relieved that Lydia had joined in, that she wasn't going to get mad at me that I had lied and included her in the lie. I was also relieved that I wasn't the only one hurt and incensed by this rejection, this not-invited reality we shared. *But Lydia, rein it in. We're not REALLY going to Italy. You can't be inviting people on a trip we're not even taking!*

"Not if it conflicts with the bar mitzvah. There is no way you are missing this bar mitzvah, Kelly. Do you KNOW the amount of hot guys that will be there? You are SO going, and you are SO walking out of there with a boyfriend. Eben did say something on the phone about you the other night. That's all I'm saying. End of discussion. Holler." Kym got up, but before she went to clear her tray, she said to me and Lydia, "No worries, though. After we snag ourselves some men, we'll totally find you guys some hotties. Well, you're taken, Stacy, but Lydia isn't. I'll scope out the joint for you."

"Thanks," Lydia said, taken aback at this sudden attention.

"No problem whatsoever," Kym said, turning her back on us quickly, and with Sara and Megan right behind her, went to get dessert. Kelly hadn't even made a dent in her lunch.

"Are you dieting?" Lydia asked.

"No, I'm just not that hungry today," Kelly responded. "Are you guys really going to Italy together?"

Lydia looked at me. I didn't want to tell Kelly that Dante and I had broken up, especially with The Chicas so close by. It might make me appear more cast out than I already felt.

"Maybe. We don't really know yet," I said, not really answering the question. "So do you wanna come over after school? Lydia and I are going to bake cookies and, you know, do stuff."

Kelly quickly looked away, then glanced up to the clock on the wall. She bit her bottom lip, and then started gnawing on her thumbnail.

"I would really love to, but I can't. I already have something to do."

"Oh," I said. "Okay."

"What are you doing?" Lydia asked.

Kym and The Chicas came back and plopped back down

with one dessert for all of us to share: green Jell-O and a brownie.

"So, four p.m.—the mall. Bar mitzvah dress shopping, we're still on? My mom will pick us up at six, and she said she'd take us to pizza!" Kym said, mouth full of brown dough and saliva.

"Yeah, sure," Kelly said, without meeting our eyes.

We stared at her, disbelieving this entire scenario.

STACY FRIEDMAN'S STATEMENT OF FURY: It's one thing to diss your friends for, like, band practice, or ballet, but it's another to diss your friends for, like, other friends.

I watched as Kym took her tray to the receiving area. This holler thing really had to go. Her vernacular was so irritating, so righteous, it made me want to hurl. The green Jell-O sloshed back and forth on her tray as she tossed it on the conveyer belt. See, I told myself, Kym makes everyone so sick even her Jell-O is green from nausea!

Megan and Sara got up and left, waving good-bye.

"I wish this bar mitzvah wasn't such a big exclusive deal and that we could all go," Kelly said. "I swear I'll take lots of pictures," she offered meekly.

Lydia and I looked at each other and then back at Kelly. Pictures? Great. Why not just torture us completely and call us from the party, hold up the phone, and let us HEAR what we're missing!

5. E Is for Excluded

Lydia and I hid inside the empty classroom next to Kelly's locker. We wanted to surprise her before she went to the mall with The Chicas.

Every couple seconds I would poke my head out of the doorway to see if she was coming. We couldn't stand not being invited, but we also couldn't stand this odd divide. We had to rebalance the situation. It was like we were on *Survivor* or something, and we were scheming to save one of our tribe mates, trying to keep her from switching over to the other side.

While waiting for Kelly, we discussed our afternoon options. Kids were streaming past the classroom and trampling down the stairs toward the street to their parents waiting in cars. The dorky kids were unlocking their bicycles. There was no sign of Kelly.

"We could start our own clothing line," I said.

"Or a blog," Lydia said.

"We could rearrange Arthur's room just to confuse him."

"We could prank call Marni Gross."

"Or collect all the things from our rooms that we don't want anymore and have a garage sale."

I leaned my head out. Kelly was coming. I motioned for Lydia, and when Kelly was close enough, Lydia and I popped out and yelled,

"Surprise!"

Kelly jumped, and the first thing she did was clutch at the E pendant, which she hadn't been wearing at lunch, that was now swaying around her neck. Then, processing the situation, she quickly tucked the necklace inside her shirt.

"Hi, ladies," Kelly said. "You scared me."

"We did?" I said, smiling brightly as if I hadn't even noticed the necklace maneuver. "Sorry."

Kelly retrieved her books from her locker and then the three of us took the stairs.

"So, you're off to the mall?" I said as casually as I could.

"Mmm-hmm," Kelly responded.

"That should be fun," Lydia said.

"Yeah, maybe," Kelly answered. "Hey, maybe they'll have party bags at the bar mitzvah. I can grab you guys a couple."

"Oh, whatever. We don't really care." I shrugged my shoulders.

"Yeah, makes no difference to us. Do it, don't do it, whatever," Lydia responded, yawning.

We pushed our way out of the school and continued to walk with Kelly, although at the end of the block, she'd have to turn right and we'd have to turn left. There wasn't much time. The fall wind was soft, and the weather was a perfect cake-frosting blue.

At the corner, when we had to part, I turned to Kelly and said, "It's not like a big deal or anything, I mean we may not even be here then, but I was thinking, maybe at the bar mitzvah, you could pass your necklace back to us. Like once you go in wearing it, you can throw it back out to me, and I'll go in wearing it and throw it back to Lydia, and then we can all go together."

Kelly swallowed hard. "I don't think I can. There's gonna be, like, security there."

"Well, maybe if we found out where the party was, we could go and see if there was some side entrance, and then we could sneak in. Maybe even like a bathroom window. Not like we really care, but it's just a thought I had."

"Oh, you guys, if you got caught it would be so embarrassing. I don't think that that's a good idea."

"Maybe you could distract the door person, and while

he wasn't looking, you could write our names on the list," I said.

"Or we could go to Rye Middle School and see if anyone's left their necklace behind, like maybe someone dropped it, and we could pick it up and then go." Lydia nodded like a bobble-head doll.

Kelly looked at a loss. She seemed like she wanted to help, but just didn't know how. I wished this wasn't so difficult.

God, I have just one little question for you:

WHY
WEREN'T
WE
INVITED?

"I'm really sorry, you guys. I didn't tell you this, but I did ask Kym if there was any possible way to get you two necklaces. But they've all been given out. I tried. I really did," Kelly said.

There was an awkward silence.

"So what are you guys gonna do after cookies?" Kelly asked, almost as if she wanted to join us. Like she was afraid she might miss out on something good. "Sell Arthur's clothes and replace them with combat boots and spike necklaces?"

Lydia and I smiled. Not a bad idea.

"Actually, I just got a call. No cookies today. We're doing this thing instead. It's no big deal."

"What's the 'thing'?" Kelly asked, sounding a bit insecure.

"We're just going into the city, to see a fashion show," I said, trying to sound as honest as I could.

"You are?" Kelly answered. "How did you . . . I mean, how are you doing that?"

"Delilah is bringing us," I lied. Delilah was my father's surgically enhanced girlfriend and I wanted nothing to do with her, but she did work in the fashion world—as an administrative assistant.

"Oh." Kelly seemed really disappointed. "Which show?"

"Marc Jacobs?" I said as if it was a question, which it kind of was, since I wasn't sure if his name was Marc Jacobs or Marc Jacob or what.

"Well, have fun, I guess."

"Oh, we will. We'll tell you all about it. We promise," Lydia said.

"Great," Kelly said.

Then we all hugged and watched Kelly walk toward the mall. I felt heavy and sort of sad.

"Well, that didn't work," I said.

"Do you think she'll have more fun with The Chicas than she has with us?"

I looked at Lydia. What a horrible thought. But I didn't have an answer. It hadn't occurred to me until just then.

6. JUST BECAUSE IT'S CAPITALIZED DOESN'T MEAN I'M SHOUTING!

DEAR GOD!

I AM A LITTLE BIT MAD. SORRY I AM YELLING, BUT WHEN YOU ARE A LITTLE BIT MAD, SOMETIMES YELLING HELPS SORT THINGS OUT! LYDIA AND I SPENT OUR ENTIRE SUMMER GETTING EIGHTH GRADE–READY. AFTER MUCH WORK AND RESOLVE (IT'S NOT EASY WEARING STRIPS OF PURIFIED WATER, GLYCERIN, HYDROGEN PEROXIDE, CARBOPOL 956, SODIUM HYDROXIDE, AND SODIUM ACID, FOR THIRTY MINUTES TWICE A DAY), WE NOW HAVE WHITE TEETH, PERFECTLY STRAIGHTENED HAIR, THE RIGHT OUTFITS—OKAY, SO WE FLUBBED THAT A LITTLE—WE HAVE EVERYTHING THAT KELLY HAS BUT WE'RE NOT INVITED TO EBEN'S BAR MITZVAH!

THE "ILLEST PARTY OF THE YEAR!!"

WHY

NOT?

Okay, I'm a little calmer now. Sorry, God. Please forgive the emotional outburst, but I've become a woman possessed. First of all, I thought Lydia and I were part of The Chicas. Well, almost part of The Chicas, for a long time, but now suddenly we're not cool enough.

So why is it that they want Kelly to hang out with them, but not us? Lydia is pretty and tall and cool and smart and fashionable and I'm cute and funny. What's the problem? We're not lepers! We're not killers! We're not animals!

Why aren't we good enough anymore?

7. Swimming Against the Snide

Instead of starting a blog, designing our first clothing line, rearranging Arthur's room, prank calling Marni Gross, or having a garage sale, Lydia and I finally decided on the one thing we really wanted to do: spy on Kelly and The Chicas at the mall.

We'd have to skulk and make sure we weren't caught spying, especially by Kelly, since after all, we were "supposed" to be on our way to New York City to see the Marc Jacob show. Or was it Jacobs?

Our first stop at the mall was the food court. If we were going to spy, we needed energy. But we also needed to be discreet, so we chose a really nasty pizza place far in the suburbs of the food court. None of our friends ever ate there, or even roamed near there. When we finished with the *festival au fromage*—that's French for cheese fest—we wiped off all crumb traces, checked each other's teeth, and headed out to begin our afternoon of reconnaissance and subterfuge

(I apologize, I'm practicing. Vocab quiz, Thursday, 2 p.m. Eng 3G).

We took the escalator upstairs and then ducked quickly into a store they'd never ever wander into: Easy Spirit. We stood in the window and watched people passing, but none of the people were Kelly or The Chicas. We snuck out and hid behind a pack of mall-walkers until we caught up with them.

They were in the corridor, on a bench, lounging, laughing and joking, text messaging, and sitting on one another's laps, like they lived there, and all these other people were just visiting. Eben and Oliver were with them. My stomach did this strange thing when I saw Oliver. You know when you're on a swing and you don't need your legs anymore because you've pumped high enough that you're just coasting on the sky? I had that feeling. Kym was sitting on the bench and Sara was massaging her back, like she was her masseuse or something.

STACY FRIEDMAN'S STATEMENT OF FACT: If you are in eighth grade you do not need a personal masseuse. Even if you are in eighth grade in Hollywood.

Megan and Kelly were sharing earphones and listening to someone's iPod. Finally, they took off the headphones, handed the iPod back to Eben, and shook their heads yes, like they were agreeing that the song he just played them was in fact as good as he said it was. Megan was playing with her E necklace. I rolled my eyes.

"Why is Megan wearing her dumb necklace at the mall? No one cares about her E necklace. No one here will even know what the E stands for," I whispered to Lydia.

"Yeah. That's really dumb."

Kym stood up and as soon as her butt left the bench, Sara and Megan stood up. They all looked at Kelly, who stood up too, but just a moment behind. They walked down the hall; Eben ran, jumped up and down, and pretended to throw a football to Oliver. Then Sara and Megan hooked arms and started to sing some song I'd never heard before. Soon Kym joined in. After a couple minutes, Kym playfully smacked Kelly, urging her to sing along, which she did. They all knew the words. Something about pink pickles and hairy unicorns. They were having a ball, and we were just standing back watching it bounce. They seemed to be having a lot more fun than I had imagined them having.

"Do you know that song?" Lydia asked me, as we ducked inside Nails by Dawn. The manicurists smiled at us, but then glared when they realized we weren't using their services, just their doorway as a cover.

"No. I've never even heard it before." Suddenly I wasn't feeling just out of the loop with Kelly, I was feeling out of the loop with the world.

"Bad Breath and the Monotones, Bad Breath and the Monotones," Eben started chanting, like he was at a rock concert swaying his lighter back and forth calling for the band to start playing. It was their band. The one they made up this summer. Of course Lydia and I wouldn't know the song, because we were never taught it. My chest tightened.

Kym kept on trying to get Oliver's attention by walking next to him. Every time he moved or rotated into a different lineup, Kym would dart in and out of people to be near him. Megan and Sara would follow her every move, like they didn't know how to survive without her. And then someone said something, we couldn't tell who, and all of them, ALL OF THEM, stopped in order to laugh. They laughed so hard, Eben fell to the ground.

"It couldn't have been that funny. I mean, Kelly's not even laughing *that* hard," Lydia said.

But from the back, we could see Kelly's shoulders bobbing up and down, and she bent over at the waist the way she did when she was belly laughing. I'd never seen her laugh so hard at someone else's jokes. Only mine.

"Let's send her a text message."

Lydia whipped out her phone and I dictated.

"Wish you could be here. Marc Jacobs says hi!" Then Lydia pressed SEND.

We stalked out of the nail salon and over to a huge potted plant. Spreading aside the ferns, we saw Eben and Kym kneel into a runner's position as if they were about to race each other, and then, seconds later, they did a quick sprint up the corridor and back. They didn't care about the fact that they were getting into people's way.

Kelly put her hand in her pocket and pulled out her phone.

"She got it!" I said.

She smiled and then started typing back to us. Until Kym grabbed her by the hand.

"Your turn!" she yelled, pulling on Kelly. Kelly put the phone back in her pocket and then knelt down to race with Eben. The two of them raced. Kelly clearly didn't put her heart into it. She sort of jogged and definitely let Eben win. But then, we couldn't even believe what happened next.

At the finish line (which was at the garbage can—all of sixty feet away), Eben gave Kelly a hug, and then when they parted, he kept his arm around her for a long minute before Kelly seemingly turned away.

Lydia and I stared at each other again.

"Oh, my God. What was that?" I asked.

"I have no idea," Lydia answered.

Kelly stopped to tie her shoe, and the group continued on. When she was done, she walked slowly, not really trying to catch up with them. She seemed on the fence, like she was with them but not part of them. Until she proved us wrong.

Kym turned around and yelled for her to hurry up, and then, suddenly, Kelly ran as fast as she could to catch up, jumping on Kym, piggyback style. Kym let out a scream, and then, when she realized who it was, twirled around with Kelly on her back and laughed and laughed. Finally, Kelly jumped off, and Kym, Sara, and Megan ran to use the bathroom, leaving the boys and Kelly looking at something in a store window.

Then Kelly turned, suddenly, as if she heard us or smelled us or even sensed us. It was as if we had called her name, which of course, we hadn't. Before we could be certain if she'd seen us or not, we leaped into action and retreated behind the column we had been peering out around. My heart was pounding. Lydia's wide-eyed expression mimicked my freaked-out internal state. "Ten . . . nine . . . eight . . . seven . . ." I counted, and then peered out from behind the wall just as Kelly was turning away, back to the shop window.

"Do you think she saw us?" I asked Lydia.

"I have no idea."

Then The Chicas came out of the bathroom, and the group continued on.

"This is no fun," I decided.

"It's just making me feel worse," Lydia said. "How can she not even be thinking about us?"

How many times in one week can a person be dumbfounded?

"Oh, my God. Are they going to go to a movie now? Are they going to keep doing things without us?"

Lydia didn't say a word. We both feared the answer, and as we stood there watching our best friend ride off on Kym's back, we felt ourselves begin to fade into the background.

8. Moving in on Mooreland

Things at school were tense while things at home were strangely untense. The past spring, I had returned home from school every day to a lonely mother who sat in her bedroom chair knitting a scarf that was so long, it could have been a driveway. But after camp ended, I returned home to a different mother—one who was blissed out, and it had nothing at all to do with knitting or handcrafts of any kind.

She had been spending a lot of time with her new boyfriend, Alan Weiss. And today, when I came home from school, they were swinging on the porch swing, doing the crossword puzzle together. I guess they were stumped, because both of them called up to Arthur (his bedroom was over the porch) for a nine-letter word for "Boeing engineer's study." Arthur stuck his head out the window and called down, "Altimetry."

I stopped halfway down the driveway, stunned by how much my life had changed in one year. Now my parents weren't just separated, they both had significant others! And we had to be nice to them. My father was living with a human-size Barbie Doll named Delilah who had picked her nose during my Torah portion at my bat mitzvah. No joke, she went nostril diving. Deep-sea fishing. Has this woman no tissues? Alan was okay, I guess. He had been Dante's host father the past year, so he got some added points for that.

I used the back door and ran up into my room. I could hear Arthur next door, stomping and grunting along with some Italian techno song. My dorky little genius brother was working on getting fit and it seemed to be, well, working. Dante had taught him how to dance last year, and Arthur had lost a lot of his blubber (the blubber had been well earned—all Arthur ate before meeting Dante was bread, rice, pasta, and ice cream). Arthur wanted to be an engineer, and he had a passion and a focus that could, at times, drive a sane person wild. Unfortunately, my mother and I were the only people he talked to, so we were the only recipients of his engineering speeches.

In my house on Lincoln Avenue, I seemed to be the only one in turmoil.

I was starving and couldn't wait for dinner. I was not in a good mood, so I stomped down the stairs to let everyone know. I hated the images I had in my head of Kelly jumping on Kym, of Kelly sharing earphones with Megan, of her bonding with these other girls. I just wanted to eat and then drown myself in television. So it was a bit of a shock to see that instead of three place settings, there were four.

I could hear my mother whistling in the kitchen. Classical music played from the nearby stereo, and I could hear a wine bottle being popped open. That was strange. My mother never had wine with dinner. I walked into the kitchen to see Mom, Alan, and Arthur all merrily setting the table, pouring wine, laughing, and being perfectly and irritatingly sociable.

"Hi, Stacy! I didn't see you come in! Alan is joining us for dinner tonight," my mother said, smiling, but with a slight anxiousness I couldn't quite place.

"Hi, Alan," I managed.

"How was school?" he asked.

STACY FRIEDMAN'S ADVICE TO ADULTS TRYING TO TALK TO KIDS: We don't want to talk about school! We want to talk about things we actually care about.

Alan sat in the chair that Dad used to sit in, which was weird to me, though Arthur didn't seem to mind. In fact, he seemed to relish this new addition. My mom was acting really odd, not like herself, and being completely saccharine, touching Alan's shoulder every two seconds to ask him if he was okay, did he want more wine? Was the fish cooked enough for him?

Did he want more beans? *What about me?* I wanted more beans. I didn't think the fish was cooked enough, and I'd like to be asked if I'm okay.

"Are you okay?" My mother suddenly turned to me.

"What?" I asked, completely annoyed. "Yes, I'm fine. Jeez. Why are you asking me that?" I snapped at her.

My mother shook her head at me and then turned back to Alan. I looked at Arthur, who took advantage of the silence and moved on from brain teasers to his newer interests. It was all he wanted to talk about these days. If you asked him a question about what book he was reading in school, he'd ask you if the aperture of the eye sockets on his robot-in-progress were inherently flawed.

"You're a finance man, Alan. Whatever happened to the invention of personal service robots? Did the funding fall through? Because I'm having one tough time trying to execute my vision without my backers demanding productivity reports." Arthur asked. So Alan did have a job. Finance. Whatever that meant.

"I think the government is still subsidizing the cost of that project. I think they might be setting their sights a bit lower than yours."

"That's a shame. But I'm not allowing technical limitations

to curb my expectations of AI. My proposed robot will fold my clothing, wash the dishes, take out the trash, clean my room, *and* talk on the phone for me. I hope after a few upgrades, it would be sophisticated enough to go to dinner parties in my stead or any other social functions, while I attend to the bigger things, like developing my civil duties as an inventor and responding to e-mails. It'll be awesome."

I looked at him. When was Arthur ever invited to anything? He had like, no friends at all. And what sixth grader had dinner parties? This is how out of touch my brother was with the ways of our generation. He imagined our social activities to be centered around crudités and champagne.

"I suppose I could even teach him how to drive. He could go to the mall for me, buy my clothes . . . maybe he could even shower for me. What do you think, Alan?"

I stopped eating and just stared at my food instead. These people were so irritating. They were trying so hard to be pleasant. But what was pleasant? There was a new man at our table, my second-best friend had dissed me, and I wasn't invited to the party of the century. Why couldn't they at least change the subject to something a little more interesting, perhaps to the topic of ME?

"I think you are a genius, Arthur," Alan said.

"My little Einstein," my mother cooed.

Arthur beamed, drank the remainder of his orange juice, and left half of his dinner unfinished on his plate. Unlike me, Arthur had willpower, whereas I just willed power. Arthur turned to me and mouthed, "I like him," about Alan.

Of course you do, dork. The man just called you a genius.

"I saw Kelly at the mall," my mother said.

I whipped around to face her, suddenly interested in this dinner conversation.

"I bumped into her as I was picking up the cheesecake. She looks fabulous!" My mother turned to Alan to explain. "Kelly is Stacy's best friend. She's a lovely girl." Then she turned back to me. "Are you friends with the girls she was with? They looked a little . . . mature," my mother said.

This made me seethe. By "mature" she meant POPULAR! I couldn't believe how much time Kelly was spending with The Chicas. We had left around five, and my mom had gone late to the mall to pick up dessert from the Cheesecake Factory. She hadn't even gotten home until around six thirty. They must have all been there for dinner or something.

"Of course I'm friends with them," I said, defensively. "Obviously, if Kelly's friends with them, then so am I."

"I'm sorry," my mother said, hurt. "I didn't know."

"Well, now you do," I said.

I pushed my chair back and excused myself while Mom gave Alan a look that said, "What's her problem?" Great. Alan got up to clear the plates. This was good, because I can't tell you how much I hate clearing plates and putting them in the dishwasher. As I headed upstairs, I heard Arthur call out, "Shelley, Alan, if you don't mind. I could do with a cup of coffee myself, please."

I stormed up to my room and put on my thinking cap. Literally. I have an official thinking cap. It was my father's incredibly worn-out New York Yankees hat, and I seemed to do some of my best thinking while wearing it. And then I did the second thing I do when I'm stressed or brainstorming: I paced on the sunken-in pacing line I had long worn into my carpet. I hated seeing Kelly with The Chicas at the mall. And worse, I hated that my mother had seen them, too.

I could never remember the difference between metaphor and analogy, but this situation was definitely one of those. There we all were: Lydia and I twenty or so feet behind Kelly. The Chicas were twenty or so feet ahead of Kelly. And Kelly was in the middle. I twisted my cap around.

There must be a way to keep Kelly from becoming the fourth Chica. Megan and Sara were okay, I actually liked them, but they did everything that Kym told them to do, and I wasn't sure that Kym had such a good heart. What if Kym took Kelly under her wing and converted her, somehow? Made her hate Lydia and me? Turned her against us? That thought made me queasy.

We could keep our eye on her during school hours, and deal with stupid trips to the mall. But what if Eben's bar mitzvah was the place that cemented their friendship? One more amazing memory they'd share together without Lydia and me. What if Eben's bar mitzvah changed everything? It was too much. I was beyond jealous. I was enraged.

I called Lydia.

"Operation Retrieve Kelly," I said as soon as she answered the phone.

"Operation Retrieve Kelly," she repeated. "Hmm. How about ORK?"

"Sounds good to me." I was relieved that Lydia didn't question it, that she must have been thinking about it also. That made me feel instantly comforted.

"What's the plan?"

"I haven't gotten there yet," I said as I pulled out the photo album I called "SLICK" (spelled SLK for Stacy, Lydia, Kelly) and flipped through an old scrapbook of the three of us. There we were at the beach; there we were at the mall; there were the black-and-white photo-strip pictures of us. This was excruciating. "But I'm worried about all the time she's been spending with Kym and The Chicas."

"Me, too."

"And now I'm even *more* worried about Eben's bar mitzvah. Do you think that Kym and Kelly will bond so much they'll become BFFs?"

"It's a possibility."

"We have to get her back," I said.

"But how?" Lydia wondered.

We were quiet for a second. I picked up a series of black-and-white Polaroids of the three of us. At a sleepover at Lydia's last year we gave each other arm tattoos (fake, of course—mine were stars, Lydia's was the sun, and Kelly's were hearts—and done with ballpoint pens), and documented the procedure should we ever need to re-create the tattoos. When we were together, we had real, original fun. There was no way that Kelly had that kind of fun with The Chicas.

"I've got it!" I announced, slamming the photo album shut.

"What?"

"Let's get her to skip the bar mitzvah."

"She'll never go for that."

"Not if she doesn't know she's going to skip it," I said, excited and feeling fast-brained.

"Huh?" Lydia was majorly confused.

"Stay with me here! If Kelly blows off the bar mitzvah, it'll be the perfect snub! Kym will see that Kelly is choosing us over her and her dumb cousin. She'll understand that *we're* more important to Kelly than she is, and that will make her back off. If Kelly chooses us over the dumb bar mitzvah, it's proof—to us, to The Chicas, to everyone—that we're the coolest things in town, not the bar mitzvah party; and voilà, our social currency skyrockets, AND we'll have our friend back!" I struggled to catch my breath.

"But how are we going to do it?" Lydia whined.

I looked around my room, grasping for some sort of sign or symbol, something that would jar my brain into genius idea mode. I shoved the photo album under my bed with my foot, and as it slid beneath the dust ruffle, it came to me.

"Let's have a sleepover. We'll do it at your house, and we'll keep Kelly up all night. She'll be so tired that she'll sleep through the bar mitzvah!"

"That's genius! But won't she be upset when she wakes up and realizes she missed it?"

"No, she'll realize that what she's missed is us, and that the sleepover made her get her priorities in order. It'll be very *Seventh Heaven*. I promise."

STACY FRIEDMAN'S STATEMENT OF FACT: Just because your little brother is a genius doesn't mean you can't be one also.

9. Our First All-Nighter

Lydia's mom didn't know exactly what we wanted at the supermarket, but since she needed to pick up some "sundries," as she called it, she was happy to chauffeur us. I grabbed a cart and ran with it, jumping on the bumper and coasting down the junk food aisle. Lydia ran in front of the cart and dumped in jumbo bags of chips of all colors and stripes. I tossed in foot-long bags of licorice, chocolate kisses, Kit Kats, candy corn (my fave), Starburst and those long packs of gum (Juicy Fruit and Big Red). Then we went to the drink aisle for liters of Coke *and* Pepsi, and then to the ice-cream aisle for, well, everything creamy.

Back in Lydia's kitchen, we scurried around before Kelly arrived. In the pantry, we pulled out Oreos and brownie mix. The plan was to give Kelly as much caffeine and sugar as possible, which would keep her up until around 3 or 4 a.m. Then we'd feed her turkey sandwiches and warm milk so she'd get very tired and sleep well into the afternoon and miss the party.

In between the food, we had planned activities to keep Kelly alert. First, using Arthur's two-way conference caller, we were going to conference call Marni Gross and Delilah, catching both of them totally off guard and confused about who called whom. Then we were going to slink down the driveway with binoculars and spy on Theo Stern, who was home from Yale for the Jewish holiday, and who Lydia had a crush on. It was kind of a lame crush. The kind you forget you have until you see the person again. But it would still be exciting. Then we were going to shoot a video of us dancing to send to MTV, and maybe even start our very own reality show. In short, we were going to have more fun than Kelly had ever had in her natural-born life.

I looked over at Lydia, who held Oreo Double Stufs in one hand and a box full of granulated sugar in the other.

"Now, we need to stagger the sugar intake. We don't want her to crash too quickly. I mean, her mother won't even let her eat sugary cereal, so we don't want to put her into a coma or anything," she reminded me.

"True. So Cokes and candy until one a.m., and then we can munch on carrots or something and then return to brownies, Oreos, and hot chocolate?"

"Perfect."

"Oh, also, I think that we should give her your bed," I said, hesitating slightly.

Lydia looked aghast. She hated sharing her bed with anyone, much less letting anyone sleep in it without her.

"Why my bed? Why can't you guys just sleep on the floor like always?"

"Because your bed is like supernaturally comfortable. When you wake up in the morning to go to school, do you want to get out of it?"

"No."

"Exactly. So should Kelly wake up at, say, seven a.m, for anything? We want the bed to hypnotize her with its luxury. She won't even consider leaving that bed to go to the bar mitzvah."

"Okay. I guess," Lydia agreed reluctantly.

We pulled out fancy plates and big mugs. Lydia unwrapped the Oreos, and I squeezed lemons into the two supersize Cokes. I opened the cupboards and found these amazing coffee candies and poured those into a little bowl. Lydia opened the refrigerator and placed the turkey strategically in the front for later. Then she found a big serving tray, and we opened all the bags of candy and dumped the Starbursts in the middle so they'd act as the centerpiece. Then we tipped the bag of chocolate kisses around the Starbursts, the licorice around the chocolate, the gum on the edge. We pulled out another tray and did the same thing with the Cheetos and Doritos, potato chips and Cheez Doodles.

The doorbell rang.

Carefully, Lydia picked up the salty platter and I picked up the sweet platter, and we marched toward the front door, slowly and steadily, as if we were getting married.

"Hi!" we both screamed.

The second I saw Kelly, I felt happy. It already felt like old times. Like how things were supposed to be. I was overcome with excitement. This was going to be the most perfect sleepover ever. There was no way Kelly would forget it. A day out with The Chicas wouldn't hold a candle to a night in with us.

"I'm so glad you guys decided not to go to Italy," Kelly said. Then she looked down at the trays and then back at us, momentarily confused.

"Wow. Is that all for us?"

"Yup," I said as I turned to Lydia and smiled. "Dig in!"

10. ORK, Accomplished!

Lydia and I turned immediately to our first planned activity: conference-calling Marni Gross.

"Okay, but after this can we go down and watch *My Super Sweet Sixteen* like we always do?" Kelly asked.

NO! We had to do different things. Memorable things. Things that would make her realize how much fun WE were.

"Sure. Of course," I said. Not meaning a word of it.

After our prank conference call hour, which was so hilarious our smile muscles hurt from laughing so much, we ran down to the kitchen to get sugar and chocolate refills.

We were flying. After finishing off the supersize Coke, Lydia decided to make coffee to see how it would taste. It was nasty, metallic and sour. So we added a bunch of milk and sugar and then it was *très delicieux* (that's French for very delicious). We were so hyper we didn't know what to do with ourselves, so at around midnight we snuck outside with the digital camera and started choreographing these hilarious dances. We were laughing so hard I almost peed in my pants, and Kelly thinks she threw up a little bit in her mouth. It was the most fun. When we went back inside, Kelly asked if we could all French-braid each other's hair like we always do, but Lydia and I convinced her to try something new that Laila taught us at camp—Flock of Seagulls. After all, this was supposed to be the perfect sleepover, worthy of special Operation ORK.

Kelly followed Lydia and me to the kitchen where we had planned a special cooking event: create new junk food. Kelly put Oreos in the toaster, and even though the smell was *divin* (French again—heavenly) it didn't do much to change the Oreo. So then we put the Oreos into a pot, poured in a scoop of ice cream and some kisses, and melted them all together. Wow, treat of all treats! It was perfection!

STACY FRIEDMAN'S RULES FOR FUN: S-u-g-a-r!

"You guys, I've missed you. Do you realize that this is the first time we've been together like this since school started?" Kelly asked, gnawing on a red licorice rope.

YES. WE HAD NOTICED. The plan was working. I knew Lydia wanted to look at me, and I wanted to look at her, but we couldn't give away just how excited we were to have Kelly back. To be US again.

"Oh, my God, you're so right!" I said.

"It's so good to be back together like this. We should have sleepovers all the time!" Lydia geniusly proposed.

"Oh, my God, let's! Let's have one every weekend. We'll switch houses," Kelly said.

YAY! Lydia and I could not have concocted a more ideal plan. It was ridiculous how easily everything was falling into place. Regular sleepovers? Laughing until dawn? Peeing in your pants? Throwing up a little in your mouth? People, everything was exactly where I wanted it. The three of us together again.

"Let's do it," I said.

"Next Friday, my house," Kelly said.

We gave each other a triple high five to cement the deal.

Then Kelly suggested we should play a game of Cranium because we were in the middle of a lifelong game. Whoever gets a million points first, wins. But we convinced her to do something more active, so we went down to the basement where Lydia had a Ping-Pong and pool table. We played four games of Ping-Pong, tried to shoot pool without knocking the balls off the table (very difficult), and played three rounds of Boggle (with a four-letter minimum), but then around one thirty a.m. Kelly yawned, so Lydia and I looked at each other and realized we needed to be on our feet, or moving, or something stimulating. The crash was imminent; that much was clear. Even though she'd been asking to watch TV and to play Cranium, we didn't want to put her on a couch for fear she'd doze off. But we couldn't keep feeding her sugar for fear she'd spiral into a fructose coma. We had to keep her alive. And then it came to me,

"Midnight swim!" I said, the lightbulb of good ideas burning bright over my head.

"Really?" Lydia asked.

"Yup. It'll be just like taking a bath. Only in a swimming pool. And outside," I said.

We held hands as we walked down to the pool house in the pitch dark. It was terrifying. Kelly's teeth were chattering from fear. Lydia jumped anytime she heard a leaf rustle. But we made it.

The water was very warm and all the lights were on so we could see each other really clearly. We had to be sort of quiet because we didn't want to wake Lydia's parents or the neighbors. We stayed in the shallow end and did handstands and tried to do cartwheels in the water (couldn't do it).

In the pool, Kelly said, "You guys, I still don't even know about camp!"

Lydia and I squealed with excitement. We really wanted Kelly to know everything that happened.

"Okay, first, you have to know all about Laila Wertheimer," I said.

"The coolest girl on earth," Lydia added.

"Totally!" I concurred and then continued, "Okay, so Laila is from L.A.—"

"She's been on movie sets—" Lydia said.

"And she's had surgery—"

"A nose job—" Lydia corrected.

"That's surgery!" I argued.

"I guess so. Anyway, she's so beautiful and cool, which is the rarest combination, and she taught us so much. . . ."

"Like about celebrities and fashion and—"

"We'll show you her picture!" Lydia said.

There was a weird short pause. We were waiting for Kelly to say something, recognize how cool we were by knowing someone as awesome as Laila, but all she said was . . .

"I wonder what time it is? We should probably go to bed. I don't want to be too tired for this bar mitzvah tomorrow."

Lydia and I looked at each other.

"Oh, it's really early, like only midnight," Lydia said.

"Really? It feels so much later," Kelly responded.

We climbed out of the pool, using the deep-end ladder, and cozied into soft, thick towels.

"Whoever's hungry raise her hand!" I said. We all raised our hands. "I know the perfect thing. I saw turkey in the refrigerator. Let's make a midnight snack of turkey sandwiches! We can pretend it's Thanksgiving leftovers!"

"Turkey sandwiches? We have turkey sandwiches? I haven't had a turkey sandwich in, wow, I don't know how long. In like forever. I love turkey sandwiches, absolutely adore them! It's been so long I was wondering if turkeys were extinct," Lydia said a little too enthusiastically. Kelly looked over at her like she was nuts.

We walked back up to the house wrapped up in our towels, shivering, and carrying our clothes. On our way to the house, Kelly started to absentmindedly hum. It sounded suspiciously like the song she and The Chicas had been singing together at the mall. That really got my goat. Not that I had any goats, but if I had, one of them would have been gotten.

"Hey, guys, what did zero say to eight?" I asked.

"What?"

"Nice belt."

It took them a second, and then they busted out laughing. In the kitchen, while I made turkey sandwiches (and attempted to get Lydia to stop doing her "Yum-yum turkey dance"), I tried to figure out a way to let Kelly know that we could have started a band this summer if we had wanted to. We just hadn't wanted to. Or maybe it was that we hadn't thought of it. Whatever the reason, we were still just as cool, and I wanted her to remember that, so I said, "Oh, Lydia, we should show Kelly the dance that we made up with Laila."

Lydia's face lit up and then fell, quickly. "We don't have the song!"

"Oh, yeah," I said, completely disappointed. The dance was so good and I wanted Kelly to see it; maybe we could even teach it to her. "Maybe we can find it online," I said hopefully.

"But we don't even know who sings it."

"That's okay," Kelly said. "You can show me another time."

"Yeah, maybe. If we ever find the song," I said.

"I'm sure it's really good," Kelly offered.

"Oh, it really is. Laila is a great dancer," Lydia said.

"Not better than you," I said. Lydia smiled, accepting the compliment. We dug into our sandwiches. Lydia excused herself to pee, but I knew she was going upstairs to fluff the pillows on her bed for Kelly.

Meanwhile, Kelly and I had a competition to see who could shove the most sandwich into our mouths. When Lydia came back down, we were choking with laughter. Tears were streaming down our faces, and turkey was falling out of our mouths.

Lydia quickly shoved her sandwich into her mouth, almost the entire thing at once, and that just did it. Kelly fell to the floor in a seizure, a laughing convulsion. I sat down; I couldn't keep myself standing up, I was laughing so hard, and Lydia just calmly chewed and swallowed, with her straight-man face, which made us laugh even harder. When we finally calmed down, Kelly said, "This has been such a fun night, you guys."

"Ohmygod . . ." we agreed, swallowing the last of the food. "Definitely."

Our eyes were getting heavy, and it was nearing four a.m. I was hoping we could stay up until at least five a.m., but we were fading fast. We headed up the stairs, drained, full, relaxed, and happy. As Lydia and I got in our sleeping bags and Kelly got in bed, we looked at the clock: 4:05 a.m. Not bad.

"God, you guys, I am so tired. I can't believe I have to wake up in four and a half hours. I'm going to be so dead," she said as she shut her eyes. Lydia turned the lights out, and as she slipped back into her sleeping bag, we smiled at each other and—slap—quietly gave each other a high five.

Bingo. It worked. We were a threesome again. Things were just how they used to be. AND there was no way Kelly would make it to Eben's bar mitzvah tomorrow. She'd oversleep, wouldn't even care, and we'd have the day for the three of us.

All to ourselves. Best Friends Forever. Tomorrow we could play Cranium and watch *Super Sweet Sixteen*, and do everything that Kelly had wanted to do tonight. We could do anything we wanted all day long. That was my last thought before falling fast and deeply asleep.

11. Duly Noted!

We woke up at ten thirty, bleary-eyed, but happy. Until we realized that Kelly wasn't in bed. Lydia looked in the bathroom, but it was empty. She ran downstairs to find her mother in her bathrobe drinking coffee and reading the paper, but she hadn't seen Kelly. By the time Lydia returned, I had already found the note on the nightstand next to Lydia's bed.

> *Hi guys! I didn't want to wake you. That was the best night ever! I only had like four hours of sleep, but I feel completely refreshed! I'm off to Bianca's to get my hair straightened and my nails done. I really wish you had been invited to this party, and I'm sorry you have to miss it, but I swear I'll call you tonight and tell you everything!*
> *Love, Kelly*

We hated the note. Especially the part that said, "I really

wish you had been invited to this party." Lydia and I were glum and sulky.

When my mother arrived, my *not good* mood turned especially bad when she reminded me that she and Alan were going canoeing up the Hudson to watch the leaves change colors. To watch the leaves change colors? How long were they planning on staying in this canoe—two months? I had to spend the day "minding" Arthur. God, my mom was so annoying.

"It's a glorious day. I feel so vibrant!" my mother sang as we drove home.

I suppose I should have been happy for her. I mean, this was a big improvement from last spring, when she had been all moody and knitty, but I wasn't.

I couldn't believe that after all the fun we'd had last night, Kelly chose to go to the bar mitzvah. After midnight swimming, a turkey-eating contest, Boggle-mania, and iron-chef–style junk-food–making experiments, she chose The Chicas over us. She'd even said, "This is the best night ever, you guys," but what? We were cool enough for last night, but not cool enough for her to skip some dumb party?

"What are your plans today with Arthur?"

"Cable."

"Stacy, it's gorgeous outside. You have to do something. I

won't let you sit inside all day. Go into town. I'll give you money for pizza."

"Whatever." What I wanted to do was go to Eben's bar mitzvah. A feeling of dread grew in my chest. What if we returned to school Monday and found we had no friends left? What if we became the losers? Or worse, what if we became the friends Kelly was embarrassed to still have? I couldn't bear this. The thought of it all made me panicky. As we pulled up to our driveway, my mother turned to me. "You know, it might be better if I stayed home with the two of you."

"Mom, we'll be fine," I said, irritated.

"I'm sure you'll be fine, but you've never stayed alone before. What if there's an emergency?"

"We'll call you," I said, as if she were some sort of idiot. I jumped out of the car, ran to my room, and called Lydia.

She was feeling just as strange as I was, and said she'd come right over. She said it might take her a while since she was walking.

I was so anxious waiting for her that I ran out onto the driveway with my cell phone just as she arrived. Lydia was out of breath and blotchy.

"What a difference a bike makes," she said. "I'm beat. I practically ran here."

I waved my big, clunky cell phone in the air. I felt frantic. "Let's call her."

"We can't just call her for no reason," Lydia said. "I mean she knows we know she's occupied. It'd be a little weird, don't you think?" She hooked her arm in mine and we walked back to the house.

I stopped, thinking. "Not if we *had* to call her. Not if there was a really important reason."

"Well, we don't have an important reason," Lydia answered, dragging me to the kitchen. Lydia and I were always hungry. She pulled out the leftover spaghetti and meatballs, and I grabbed some raw cookie-dough mix, and we ate while we plotted.

"But we have an important reason."

"And that is . . . ?" Lydia asked.

I looked around the kitchen, trying to jog my imagination. My eyes skidded over a phone book, the kitchen table, the toaster, a Cuisinart, pot holders, cookbooks, a coffeemaker, and a notepad next to the phone. Aha!

"Her pen! A few months ago she left her pen here!"

"I hate to point out the obvious, but I'm almost certain that in those few months, Kelly has found herself a new pen."

"Okay, so we don't have a real reason, but let's call her anyway. Let's call her and see if maybe she wants to leave and come over here, with us!" I said.

Lydia shook her head. "But you can't call her. They're in the middle of the services."

"Well, I called you in the middle of my service, didn't I?"

"But that was different. You wanted to tell me to come, not tell me to leave."

"True."

Lydia and I stared at each other and then I flipped open my phone and held down the number 2—Kelly's number on speed dial.

I wasn't sure what I was going to say, but assumed I'd find the words once I heard her voice. Only it went straight to her voice mail, and I flipped the phone closed.

My mother came into the kitchen to kiss me good-bye and give me a hundred and forty-five emergency phone numbers. I swear there was even one for Dr. Hubert, the local veterinarian, and we didn't even own any pets.

"Okay, bye, have fun," I said, not even looking at her, too distracted by my racing thoughts about Kelly.

"You know, I think perhaps, I won't go," my mother said. "What if the fire alarm accidentally goes off? Or the smoke alarm? You kids won't know what to do," she said wringing her hands.

"Mom, the alarms have never accidentally gone off before. Now go, you're making me anxious," I said.

My mother bent down and kissed me good-bye and then, as if she was still unconvinced, walked very slowly out of the kitchen and toward her date with Alan Weiss.

We went to my room, passing Arthur in his, tinkering with a shopping cart that appeared to have a tinfoil head. A disassembled vacuum cleaner was lying nearby. He was adjusting some wires, and then he clapped twice, like the contraption was a light he was trying to turn on and off. Nothing happened. Lydia and I shrugged at each other; we had no idea what this kid was doing. We went to my room and tried Kelly one more time. Voice mail. Again.

"Did we say something wrong?"

Arthur ran down the hall and downstairs.

"No, I don't think so," Lydia said.

"Then what? Why not us?" I asked.

Lydia looked up at me. "Maybe we're not cool enough for them," she said.

I stamped my foot like a child about to have a tantrum. "But we ARE cool!"

Arthur returned from downstairs, trailing a large piece of sheet metal in one hand, wearing a tool belt around his waist, and carrying Dad's old fishing-tackle box in the other. I shook my head at him. Poor Arthur. He was all brain, some brawn, but no brass. I wondered if he'd ever get the necessary confidence to leave his broken robots behind and make some friends.

I turned to Lydia. "If they don't think we're cool enough to get an invitation, we need to make them see just how wrong they are. Then they'll feel so bad that they'll grovel at our feet with apologies, and beg our forgiveness. We have to out-cool them."

"But how in the world are we possibly going to do that?" Lydia asked.

We went back down to the kitchen to eat while we thought. Arthur kept traipsing back and forth. Once from the garage with lumber, another time from the basement with old suitcases. By the time he was rustling around for garbage bags under the sink, he was visibly sweating.

"Arthur, what are you doing?" I asked.

"Trying to make my robot work," he said.

"With all that stuff?"

"Yes. I need lumber for the base, sheet metal for the body, a garbage bag for the inflatable breathing apparatus. And on and on. Why? You want to help me?" he asked hopefully.

"No thanks. We have things to do."

He looked at me and then at Lydia, just sitting there at the kitchen table, our chins propped lazily in our hands. We had been squeezing out cookie-dough mix and eating it straight from its sausage-shaped casing. We had also completely devoured the leftover pasta and meatballs. Cold.

"Yeah. You look busy," he said.

"We're thinking," Lydia told him, defensively.

"What about?"

"Nothing that would interest you, Arthur," I said, a bit snidely.

"Fine. Don't include me!" He stormed away, and when he came back, he passed by without even looking at us, but we looked at him. He was carrying an apple crate filled with discarded metal remnants of all different shapes and sizes.

"Arthur!" I shouted, alarmed at the level of my voice. He didn't turn, he just stopped and stared straight ahead.

"What?" he said.

"What's in that box?" I asked, standing up. Lydia looked at me like I was nutso.

"Parts."

We followed Arthur upstairs. Lydia was ahead of me, and she turned around and made the "What-are-we-doing?" face. I gave her back the "You'll see" face.

When we got to his bedroom, my heart began to race as I saw, lying on top of his workbench, hundreds upon hundreds of scrap pieces of metal cut into letters. His welding material and goggles were pulled out, waiting to be utilized. Lydia didn't have to ask me again what was going on. She was already on the same page.

"Oh, my God," she said.

We knew what we had to do.

We angled ourselves at the workbench, Lydia by the large vise and me next to the eight-drawer stack of nails, and started sifting frantically through all the pieces of metal.

"Hey! What are you doing?" Arthur asked.

"Looking for E's! Get over here and look!" I demanded like some sort of overbearing stage mother.

"I'm not using any E's. My robot's name is Oman Hudi, it doesn't have an E in it," he answered.

"What does that even mean?" I asked, gripping two fistfuls of metal.

"Nothing. It's an anagram for humanoid," he said, very pleased with himself.

Lydia and I turned our attention back to the workbench and rifled through the remaining letters.

"I was going to name him, 'Arthur's first humanoid,' but that felt too stuffy, then I was thinking of calling him 'Boris the—'"

"Arthur, please just help us!"

Arthur walked over and started sifting through all the letters he had, and then he looked up at both of us and said, "Why are we doing this?"

"We're crashing a bar mitzvah," I said.

"Why would you want to do that?"

"The party, Arthur, we're crashing the party, not the service," I responded.

"Oh," he said and then continued digging. He stopped, looked up again.

"And why do you want to do that?"

I sighed, rolled my eyes, and quickly explained the concept of fun to my socially arrested brother.

"But why the E?"

He was asking too many questions, and Lydia threw herself onto her knees, salivating over the scraps.

"Necklaces," Lydia said, frantic, breathless, racing against the clock.

"The invitations to get in are E necklaces. WE NEED E'S!" I shouted.

"I have soldering, welding, and brazing tools. Why don't we just make the E necklaces out of these scraps?" Arthur asked.

Lydia and I stopped sifting. We looked at each other, eyes bulging. Genius.

He continued. "According to diynetwork.com, brazing uses lower temperatures than welding but higher temperatures than soldering, and it creates a stronger bond than soldering."

"What about chains?"

Arthur reached his hand into a box and pulled out a fistful of chains.

"Just for the record, I bought these to be used as links for fluid movement for Oman Hudi. Not as necklaces."

"Wait! We can't just walk in with these necklaces when everyone knows we weren't invited," Lydia said.

I clutched the odd-shaped metal piece to my heart and thought for a minute. She was right. We couldn't just walk in there when everyone in our entire social network knew we hadn't been given necklaces. That'd be such a Marni Gross thing to do. I was stumped.

I stared at Oman Hudi while thinking. I sat down on Arthur's mangy, unmade, twin-size bed, trying to come up with some sort of plan. I looked at the tools, the sheet metal, the drop cloth and paint cans that Arthur had strewn around the room. Arthur had started with nothing and was creating something. Using tinfoil and a shopping cart, Arthur was building a brand-new identity.

"You know how I said we needed to out-cool them?"

"Yeah?"

"Well, we're still going to, but on top of that, we're also going to outsmart them. All of them. We're going to have everyone at that bar mitzvah clamoring to be our friend. And then, once they're where we want them, you know what we'll do?"

"What?" Lydia wanted to know.

"What?" Arthur asked, now intrigued.

"When they least expect it, we're going show them that we've been one step ahead of them the whole time. We'll be the girls who can't stop receiving invitations, the girls all the other girls want to go to the mall with. We'll be the Big Girls On Campus."

"But how? How?" Lydia asked.

I took in a long drink of air for dramatic effect; I had Arthur and Lydia wrapped around my pinkie. Hell, I had them wrapped around my entire forearm.

"Disguises," I answered.

"Disguises," Arthur repeated, seemingly impressed.

"Disguises," Lydia said, as if the word was new in her mouth and had a chocolatey taste, oh so delicious.

12. Running out of Time (and Money!)

The three of us sat in a row on our heels staring at the brazing iron and glue gun that lay on the workbench. Arthur's rug had so much hot glue and wood chip residue, Lydia and I had to pull our long boho skirts over our knees to be comfortable.

"Sheet metal," Arthur said, his open palm extended toward Lydia and waiting.

I passed the small misshapen piece of sheet metal to Lydia, who placed it in Arthur's hand. "Sheet metal," Lydia repeated, like she was the surgical nurse.

"Gloves," Arthur said.

I passed the thick carpenter gloves to Lydia, who placed them in Arthur's hand. "Gloves," Lydia repeated.

"Dovetail metal cutter," Arthur demanded.

Lydia and I scanned the tools, but didn't know what that meant. Arthur used his chin to motion toward an evil-looking pair of scissors. I picked it up and handed it to

Lydia, who placed it in Arthur's palm with an audible *thwak*.

Arthur waited.

"Dovetail metal cutter," Lydia said, quickly remembering her role.

Arthur pulled the goggles over his head, started up the brazing iron, and went to work. In less than five minutes we had one perfect E necklace. I handed Lydia another sheet metal piece and she handed it to Arthur, who pulled his goggles back down and made another one. He held it up to the light and smiled at his handiwork.

"There you go, ladies, two perfectly made E necklaces."

"We need one more," I said. "Actually, not a necklace, but a pin. For a lapel."

"For who?" Lydia asked.

"Yeah, for who?" Arthur asked.

"Just a friend. We're meeting him there."

Lydia gave me a strange look and I winked, kind of, but she still didn't seem to get it. Arthur made one more *E* and mounted it on a sharp tack. We used an eraser head as a backing. I glanced up at the clock. We were running out of time.

We headed to my bedroom to start getting dressed when Lydia turned to me. "Oh, no! Stace! These are silver. Eben handed out gold E's."

I stopped in my tracks and then we ran back to Arthur, thrusting the E's at him.

"Make them gold, make them gold," I shrieked, starting to panic because we were really running behind now. Arthur, a sponge in tense situations, started to turn red. My frenetic energy was making him anxious. He started running around his room looking for something with which he could turn silver to gold. He was bumping into things: his desk, his closet door. He was like a dog who'd been blindfolded. Finally, he found gold spray paint and gold glitter in an old art box on the top shelf of his supply closet.

"You spray. And get dressed," I said, and Lydia and I flew back into my bedroom.

"Where am I going?" Arthur called from his bedroom. As we pulled all my clothes out of the closet, I yelled back, "Put on your nice suit. You're coming with us." I dumped all my clothes on my bed.

"I'm not going to any dumb party! I have work to do. I have a patent to apply for!" he shrieked from the other room.

"GET DRESSED NOW, ARTHUR SAUL FRIED-MAN!"

Lydia looked at me.

"STACY!!" Arthur yelled back, mortified.

"Saul?" Lydia mouthed. I shrugged. We pulled through

my clothes, and then stared at them with disdain.

"Where's all your fall fashion?" Lydia asked.

"I don't have fall fancy, yet! Only fall casual!" I shrieked.

"What in the world are we going to do?" Lydia asked.

Arthur walked into my room and glared at me.

"Arthur, please go put on your nice suit."

"Stacy, I'm not coming! I have too much going on here to abandon it for a cause that's not even my own!"

This was an emergency. In emergencies you were supposed to remain calm.

"Arthur," I began, grappling for what I was going to say that would get him to the bar mitzvah without kicking and screaming. "I don't think you understand. This is an animatronics themed bar mitzvah. Everything at the bar mitzvah party has a robotics theme. There will be patent officials there. People from NASA will be there. Someone representing the Japanese Robot Research Lab will be there" (I really hoped that was the name. Arthur had mentioned it once in passing). "You'll be in heaven. You can network. Maybe even get some government subsidies for Oman Hudi," I said calmly, but feeling absolutely desperate. Mom would kill me if I left Arthur home alone. I was babysitting. I think it was even illegal to leave him—I had no choice.

Arthur was starry-eyed.

"Really?" he asked.

"Really," Lydia and I said in unison.

Arthur ran out of my bedroom, and Lydia and I shrugged at each other. Before our shoulders even dropped from the shrug, Arthur had returned wearing his nice suit. The only problem was, it was enormous. He had lost so much weight he looked like he was wearing our father's suit.

"Look, Lydia, a suit with a boy in it," I said.

"What do I do?" Arthur whined.

I held up a very outdated *Little House on the Prairie* influenced dress from Urban Outfitters. "This isn't much better? Yours is too big and mine is too old."

"Let's go to the mall!" Arthur suggested.

Lydia's eyes lit up. "Okay, so we'll bike there fast, grab some outfits, and then head over to the synagogue."

"Bikes?" I asked.

"Silver Rush!" Lydia said.

"A car service! Okay, that could work," I agreed.

"But what about disguises?" Lydia asked.

"Let's go to Dad's!" Arthur answered.

I looked at him, confused. "Dad's? Why there?"

Arthur pretended to stick his finger up his nose and go scrounging.

"DELILAH!" I screamed. It was perfect! "We'll go through her accessories, she's got everything. Even wigs. All the designers send her everything before it even comes out."

"But where are we going to get the money for the mall? For Silver Rush?" Lydia asked.

"Mom gave us money for pizza!" Arthur offered.

"That's only twenty dollars, Arthur."

We all flopped down on my bed to think. I crossed my arms across my chest. I looked searchingly at my desk, my pink-and-green polka-dot wallpaper, my much in need of updating wardrobe. Then I spotted my dollhouse.

My dollhouse.

Arthur saw my eyes linger. He shook his head no.

I ignored him, got up, walked over and knelt down beside it.

STACY FRIEDMAN'S STATEMENT OF FACT: Sometimes the smartest ideas are also the hardest to bear.

"Stacy, I don't think this is a good idea," Arthur said, as I reached my hand into the back of the little girl's bedroom and pulled out a thick envelope filled with cash.

"What in the world is that?" Lydia asked.

"My bat mitzvah money," I answered.

Lydia threw her hands up. "Oh, Stacy, you can't do that!"

"What choice do we have? It's either that or stay here while everyone is at a party without us. Kym could sink her fake nails deeper into Kelly. If we're left out of this, there's no telling what else we'll be left out of. Come Monday, we could be inconsequential."

Lydia folded her arms across her chest and then refolded them the other way.

"Okay. Let's do it."

Arthur called the car service, and Lydia and I tossed some of my mother's makeup into my canvas messenger bag. A horn gave out three quick, short honks, and we ran out of the house and scooted into the back of the waiting car.

"We're making three stops," I told the driver. "And if you could wait for us at two of the stops, we'll give you a really big tip!"

The driver turned around. He was chewing on a toothpick and was wearing a Mets baseball cap, backward. I could see my reflection in his mirrored glasses. I looked like a Tootsie Pop in the image.

"A big tip, huh?" he asked, amused. "I'd like to see that."

I glanced at his ID on the back of the plastic divider. It was a very nice photo, actually, although he was wearing the exact same outfit today as he was in the picture: the baseball hat, and a T-shirt that said, I ♥ THE METS. Underneath, was his name: Jesus Ferguson.

"Oh, we'll tip you, Jesus. Trust me."

Jesus turned around again, smiling tightly, so we couldn't see his teeth.

"It's pronounced 'Hey-Zeus.' It's Spanish."

I shrunk a little bit in the seat. "Sorry," I said meekly.

And then he stepped on it, almost like he knew we had only little over an hour to find a dress, go through Delilah's closet, and get to the synagogue before everyone left for the evening's main event: the Oscar-themed bar mitzvah.

Jesus had barely pulled up at the mall before we bounded out of the backseat. We ran up the escalator and tore through the racks at Neiman Marcus. I went right for an embroidered medallion dress, and Lydia went directly for a lace-print strapless dress. On our way to the cash register, I realized we still needed to get Arthur an outfit.

"Arthur, run down to Thrifty's Lot and get a pair of jeans and a concert T-shirt."

"For who?" he asked.

"For you!" I said.

"Oh, no. I'm not dressing like some grade-C beatnik. I'm happy to just wear this," he said looking down at his everyday outfit (I swear he must have cut some sort of promotional deal with L.L. Bean). His rumpled, blue buttoned-down oxford shirt was tucked into dusty olive-colored, oil-stained Rangeley chinos. Over that he wore a beige tropic-weight blazer that didn't fit. And on his feet were rustic penny loafers, which he loved because he could wear them year-round.

"Arthur, you need to dress in disguise. We can't be found out. Everyone knows how you dress, and NO ONE ELSE dresses like you. No one else who doesn't have a day job trading options on Wall Street. Now go, before we miss the animatronics display." I handed him forty dollars, and Lydia and I went to the cashier to pay. Total price: $350. Yikes. Lydia and I gulped. The counter woman looked at us.

"Is there a problem?" she asked.

"No, just . . . trying to find my money," I said, pulling out my bat mitzvah envelope from my knapsack and handing her every last cent. We found Arthur in front of Radio Shack. Luckily, that was right next door to Hot Topic, so we ducked in and bought Arthur some electric blue temporary hair color, too.

We jumped back into the waiting cab, and Arthur handed Jesus ten more dollars. We gave him our next address, and we were on our way. In a few minutes, we pulled up to Dad's house, told Jesus we wouldn't be long, and ran to the front door. Arthur rang the bell, and within two seconds, as if she were expecting company, Delilah opened the front door. She had self-tanner streaks on the sides of her neck and was drinking Diet Pepsi out of the can with a straw.

"Hi, kids, this isn't your weekend with us, is it?" she asked, confused. Delilah ALWAYS looked confused, but her forehead never puckered. When she spoke, her cheeks didn't move. She was the poster girl for postcosmetic surgery.

"No, but you know how you're always asking me if I want to borrow some of your jewelry?"

"My jewelry? Yes, I think so," she answered, still confused.

"Good, because we, I mean I, was invited to this party and I have absolutely no accessories, so I was wondering, could I have a peek in your closet?"

"Why sure, Stacy!" Delilah said as if we were the only visitors she'd ever received in her life. She opened the door and we all walked in. She turned her head and yelled at the top of her lungs,

"MORTY! COME AND LOOK WHO'S HERE!" A few seconds later, there were footsteps, and then a few seconds after that, my dad. When he saw it was us, his hand reached up and he folded down the collar on his Izod. Was my old man popping his collar?

"Well, what a nice surprise," my dad said, kissing Arthur and me on our foreheads. "Hello, Lydia."

"Hi, Dr. Friedman."

"And to what do we owe this pleasure?"

"Stacy wants to borrow some of my jewelry!" Delilah exclaimed, as excited as if I had dropped a sack filled with hundreds at her feet.

"Well," my dad said proudly, putting his arm around her, "isn't that something? Isn't that nice?"

"Okay, so we're gonna go upstairs now," I said.

"I'll stay here, I'd like to tell Dad and Delilah about Oman Hudi," Arthur said.

Lydia and I raced upstairs and threw open Delilah's closet door. It was ginormous. You could walk right in and everything. There was a wall that was just mirror and plenty of space to stand back and investigate your chosen outfit. We went through her gold necklaces, bangles, hoop earrings, and hair extensions.

"This!" I said and held up a wig of long, loose blond curls; it was just the kind of hair I had always wanted and the way that Kelly and The Chicas wore their hair.

"Oh, my God! Perfect!" Lydia said.

"And these!" I held up some gold earrings—two C's in opposite directions.

"Very British *Vogue!*" Lydia said. "What about me?"

I dug through the basket filled with scarves and hats. I pulled out a leather page-boy cap.

"How about this?"

"No, I'll look like a street urchin from *Oliver Twist*."

I dug further. I pulled out another wig, but this one was shorter and curlier.

"What about this?" I asked.

"Ooohhh, I've always wanted curly hair," she said, trying it on. She looked much better curly than I did. I put my wig on. We were totally different from ourselves. The wigs were very good. They didn't seem wiggy.

I did her makeup, giving her a light dusting—a soft mermaid type of look, and she did the same to me. Then I grabbed a delicate cream-colored lace scarf, and she wrapped it loosely around her neck. When we stood back, what we saw amazed even ourselves. We resembled an ad campaign for something wistful and elusive, something hard to reach or put your finger on. Yes, we looked like models in a perfume commercial.

We ran downstairs. "ARTHUR, get your groove on! We're late! Meet us outside, stat. Bye, Delilah and Dad! Love you! See you later!" We slammed out the front door, ran down the driveway, and jumped into the backseat of the car.

A minute later, Lydia and I did everything in our power not

to have a spleen explosion from laughter. Arthur walked out in a tight black T-shirt that said, in white letters, RAMONES across the chest; a pair of dark jeans; and Puma sneakers. He had put mousse in his hair, along with the blue spray, but hadn't fully rubbed it in, so his head looked like a little diorama of the sky. I rubbed it in, wiped the laugh-tears from my eyes, and we all pressed on.

13. So This Guy Walks into a Synagogue . . .

The actual bar mitzvah ceremony was most likely coming to an end, and we were bouncing our legs up and down in the back of the car. Jesus was going way too slowly. He was driving with one hand on the steering wheel, enjoying the scenery. The guy was too relaxed. We had a party to crash—step on it, please!

"Does your wig itch?" Lydia asked, her hand rubbing her wig back and forth over her scalp.

"Terribly," I answered.

"This is really stupid. Girls are really strange. I just care about robots. Not this popularity campaign! Hey! That rhymed!" Arthur said.

I smiled a little bit, but Arthur just didn't get it. He couldn't. His only friends were made of metal and pro-grammed to like him.

We passed the bowling alley, drove straight through Rye, past the bookstore, up a hill, and finally, we coasted down a long one-lane street, where we pulled into the Mamaroneck

Jewish Center parking lot and stopped. We unfolded the remaining cash we had. We were a dollar short, but Jesus was very nice. He waved at us as he drove away; clearly amused at whatever it was we were up to.

We took a bunch of deep long breaths. I fidgeted with my wig, trying to get it to feel more in place. Something else felt off, too. Something that had nothing to do with our disguises. But at that moment, I couldn't put my finger on it.

I stared at the synagogue as I swiped at my forehead with the back of my hand. It was a lot more modern looking than ours and less homey. I straightened my outfit and Lydia straightened hers, and then I went into my bag and pulled out the two E necklaces, which we gently put over our heads. I longed to fiddle with mine, like Kelly and The Chicas seemed to do all the time, but I was afraid the gold spray paint and glitter would come off. Arthur pinned his E onto his shirt collar.

"Now you're dressing me like a Crip," he complained.

Two steps toward the synagogue, and I realized what seemed not right. I glanced around frantically.

"Oh, my God, you guys," I said.

"What? What?" Lydia turned around and asked.

"We missed it. All the cars are gone."

Both Lydia and Arthur turned and looked around, taking

in what we had so clearly missed. The parking lot was totally empty.

A lump formed in the back of my throat, and I swallowed hard to get rid of it. We had gone through all this for nothing? I had spent my bat mitzvah money for an empty parking lot? Lydia was frighteningly pale and panicked.

"What about the patent officials?" Arthur yelled. "You made me dress like a member of the *Real World* and I'm not even going to meet the NASA people? I'll never get a grant now!"

"Maybe they're inside," Lydia said hopefully. "Maybe the parents just dropped all the kids off and are going to pick them up when it's over."

I was dubious, but we walked up the synagogue steps and opened the heavy doors. We took a few steps inside and the echo of our feet was the loudest sound in there. We entered the assembly room, and it was empty. I could hear our sighs of defeat before we even breathed them. Light streamed down through the windows and onto the benches and the bema, but we were the only ones there to see it.

I sat down in one of the pews and looked around. We were stuck. Truly stuck. We had no money, no bikes, no mode of transportation. Jesus was already long gone. With a wave and a shout of "Good luck!" he had driven off to pick up his next passenger. There was no possible way we'd be able to walk home from here. Now we wouldn't be able to go to the party OR get home.

Lydia turned to me.

"Well, what now?"

Just then the synagogue doors opened. When I saw who it was, my mouth formed the shape of the O, and I had to catch myself before I blurted out his name. Oliver.

My hand was still on my wig, but I adjusted it so I looked like I was playing with my bangs. I hoped he didn't recognize me. We hadn't thought of what would happen if someone *did* recognize us. What were we supposed to say? *It's the strangest thing—I was walking down the street and this wig just fell on my head!?*

He looked at all of us and smiled shyly and said hi in a way that suggested we were unfamiliar to him. His hair was neatly combed and his suit was casual, yet fancy, but most of all, it fit him. He cleaned up nice. Oliver walked down the aisle, searched a few pews, got down on his knees, peered on the ground, and seemingly disappeared. A few seconds later he emerged, triumphant. He held a small dark umbrella and headed back toward us.

"My mom forgot her umbrella," he explained and rushed to the doors.

"Hey, mister. Wait!" I called, slightly mortified that I had just called a boy my age mister. What was wrong with me?

He turned and smiling said, "Yes, missus?"

I smiled, relieved.

"Well, we were supposed to be at the bar mitzvah but events unforeseeable to us occurred, and now we need to get to the party, but since we forgot our official invitations with the address on it, we can't exactly seem to get there."

I pulled the E necklace out from under my dress proving my validity. Lydia did the same.

"What about him?" Oliver pointed to Arthur.

Arthur pointed at his E pin. "I'm in and out. I don't go in for this type of social frenzy. I'm just here on a business venture. Although the project is topical, I'm going to decline sharing its specific nature. Suffice it to say, it's in the name of a patent."

Oliver looked utterly befuddled by this little non sequitur speech.

"I have no idea who he is," I said to Oliver. "He must have wandered away from high-IQ camp. We found him hitching a ride off the freeway."

"Yeah, the woman inside that car in the parking lot," Oliver said, playing along, "not really my mother. She's just playing the part until she gets a better-paying job. And speaking of better-paying jobs, her meter is running. Do you guys want a lift over to the party?"

"Yeah, that'd be great, thanks," I said, trying not to let on just how relieved I was.

"Yeah, thanks," Lydia said.

Arthur shrugged.

I squeezed Lydia's hand. Was this guy great or what? He was so cute! He went to look for his mother's umbrella without complaining! He was funny! And best of all, he was friends with Eben. He was our instant in.

In the car he introduced his mom and then told us his name was Oliver Solomon, which I already knew and had to pretend like I was hearing it for the first time. I also had to act like I didn't know he went to middle school with Eben.

"How do you guys know Eben?" Oliver asked us.

Uh-oh. We weren't exactly prepared for this part, either. Lydia and I stole looks at each other. We had picked out our disguises, but we hadn't come up with our stories.

"I'm an old camp friend," I lied breezily, gazing out the window at the highway.

"Did you go to Meadow Lake?" Oliver's mother asked me, through the rearview mirror.

"Yup. That's the one. One and the same. Meadow Lake."

"Oliver almost went there, but at the last minute his father decided he should go to tennis camp."

Thank GOD.

"So," Oliver said. "Are you guys from Rye? Do you know Kym Armstrong and those girls?"

Lydia mugged at Oliver big time. She gave some overexaggerated thinking faces, like *Kym Armstrong . . . Name rings a bell, but nope, nope, can't place her.* "Never heard of her," Lydia finally said.

"Kym? No. Not sure who that is. We're not from this town," I added.

"Oh, where are you from?" his mother asked through the rearview mirror again.

"Um . . . New York?" I asked-answered.

"Whereabouts?"

"In the city," Lydia answered for us all.

"Uptown or down?" the mother continued.

This was getting ridiculous. I was sweating, and now my wig was starting to itch again. Uptown, downtown? What was the difference?

"We're not really supposed to give away our address," Arthur said, coming to the rescue. "But we live in midtown, actually. Fifty-seventh Street between Lexington and Third." I almost laughed out loud when Arthur said this. The only reason he knew that address was because that's where Hammacher Schlemmer was, one of his favorite gadget and invention stores.

"Hey, I didn't even ask you. What are your names?" Oliver asked suddenly.

There was a short silence, while we all scrambled, and then I mustered the strength to tell yet another lie. "I'm Winnie . . . Winnie Foster," I said, trying to be somewhat cool and aloof—Kym style.

Arthur and Lydia both turned to me. Through my hard stare, I sent them both the following telepathic message: *It was the only name that came to mind. So what if she was the main character in my absolute favorite book in the world,* Tuck Everlasting? *It was less obvious than Betty Friedan, whose name, I'll have you know, was on the tip of my tongue.*

"Sarah Jessica Simpson," Lydia said, extending her hand.

"That sounds almost famous," Oliver said.

Arthur rolled his eyes. He did not want to play this game.

"What grade are you in?" Oliver asked me.

"Eighth," we both answered.

Arthur said, "I could pass for eighth." He paused. "I'm Arthur," he added grudgingly.

"Did you have a bat mitzvah?" he asked me.

"Yeah—last year. It wasn't such a big deal. You know. You've seen one bat mitzvah, you've seen them all," I said, trying to sound world-weary.

"Yeah, no big deal. I mean there were some stars there, and what have you, but overall, we prefer other things," Lydia said.

Oliver turned back to me.

"Are you on MySpace?"

"I don't have much time for that kind of thing. I'm big into the comedy scene. I'm training to be a comedian, so I check out the comedy clubs as often as I can . . . you know, to sniff out the competition. I'm really good friends with some of the top comics working in New York today."

What was I doing? I was thirteen, for God's sake. What thirteen-year-old was running around New York City on her own going to comedy clubs and hanging out with seasoned professionals? I was so busted.

Oliver's mother glanced back at us in the rearview mirror. Her brow furrowed, the corner of her mouth pulsed. She was on to us. I braced for the worst.

"I LOVE comedy. Don't I love comedy, Mom?" Oliver asked her.

His mother answered, "He loves comedy."

"You should check MySpace out. I'm like obsessed. It's a true problem, I was thinking of going to MySpace Anonymous, but there's no chapter in Rye."

I giggled. Oh, my word, he was so adorable. "Sure, maybe. I mean, if I have time."

Oliver nodded knowingly. "I have a feeling you'll find the time."

I felt bad lying to Oliver. Was I going to have to keep up this charade forever? Of course, I could officially change my name. Which I know for a fact people do. Was Marilyn Manson a real name? Was Dewey Decimal a real name? So what if I needed a reason to change my name? *The reason,* I imagined myself saying to the judge, as I stared up at him in his black robe holding on to the gavel; *well, the reason, Your Judgeship, is a heartthrob eighth grader who goes by the name Oliver Solomon. You have to understand, we're meant to be together. He loves comedy. Even his mother said so.*

"Yeah," I said. "I'll check it out." I gave Lydia my supercool smile. She gave me hers back—a half smirk, but her eyes twinkled. We were righteous. This was going to be the best bar mitzvah party ever. I could just feel it.

14. Bash Mitzvah

When we arrived at the entrance to the ballroom at the Mamaroneck Beach and Yacht Club, we were overcome by all the commotion. There was an actual red carpet. And big Klieg lights flanking both sides of the red velvet ropes. In gold script the words, "Eben's Academy Awards Bar Mitzvah!" were painted onto the red carpet. There was a movie marquee overhead, and in black tiled letters, an announcement of Eben's entrance into adulthood. Planted on either side of the velvet ropes were fake paparazzi (who, we learned later, were interns who worked for Eben's father) hired to snap our picture. At the end of the red carpet were two security guards flanked by two life-size statuettes of Oscar. It was amazing, unlike anything we'd ever seen, and it actually felt like the real thing. I turned around and saw Oliver's expression, which was equally as stunned as ours. But Arthur? He was unfazed, as if he walked down the red carpet every day of his life.

"This is not an animatronics-themed bar mitzvah, Stacy. You lied to me," Arthur hissed in my ear.

"I'm sorry, Arthur. I had to. We were the only people not invited out of our whole group of friends. We're on a mission. Besides, I'm babysitting you, so you have to do what I say."

"This is really unfair. Have you ever heard of Karmic revenge?"

"The band?" I asked, facetiously. Arthur turned away from me with his "harrumph!" face.

I don't know if Arthur bought it, but there was no time for further explaining. Oliver motioned for Lydia and me to walk. So we held hands as we began our march.

Flashbulbs started going off. We could hear the party raging inside.

"Over here, girls!"

"No, over here!"

"Girls! This way! Over here!"

The fake paparazzi was yelling at us, and although it was a bit overwhelming, Lydia and I strutted our stuff. We catwalked just like we had seen Tyra Banks do on *America's Next Top Model*. We lifted our knees high like we were in a marching band, slamming one foot directly in front of the other, heel in front of toe, hips swaggering side to side. We stopped every few steps and pivoted, turning and posing for a different photographer, then paraded a little bit farther. We felt famous and so naturally, we acted famous. It was amazing. We were movie stars. We were supermodels. We were model stars.

Oliver and Arthur walked behind us, Oliver with his head down and hands stuffed into his pants. He was blushing and had this funny smile on his face, which was less a smile of happiness, and more a smile of personal embarrassment. Arthur was blasé, nonchalant. He stopped and posed for only one photographer, citing later that he resembled the famous inventor, Louis Braille. Arthur did it with such ease and grace that I began to wonder if he'd been sneaking out late at night to hang out with celebrities and supermodels. But the truth was, Arthur just didn't care about this kind of stuff. Popularity, celebrity, those things didn't interest him like they did Lydia and me and nearly every single other breathing person in the world. He was immune.

As we passed the two brawny bodyguard types in the entrance, Lydia and I took a deep breath and flashed our E necklaces. One gave the nod of approval, and we made our way farther inside. Lydia and I clutched each other and just sort of spastically giggled and made other weird sounds. We'd made it. We'd crashed Eben's bar mitzvah.

On our way through the doors, we passed a wicker basket filled with suede and patterned yarmulkes, left seemingly untouched. Oliver grabbed one and fastened it in place on his head. As did Arthur. I smiled at them both, touched by the observance.

Now I understood all the hype. It was the most insane party I'd ever seen. There were women and men in black tuxedos. They were running around with headsets and walkie-talkies.

In the center of the room were life-size gold statues of the Jolie-Pitt family, all the kids were represented: Maddox, Zahara, and Shiloh. Kids were standing near them, poking, pulling, and chipping them with plastic knives and then putting the pieces into their mouths.

"Are they eating Brad Pitt?" I asked.

"It's chocolate," Arthur answered, pissy.

"How do you know?"

"When you are deprived of food you become hypersensitive to smells," he responded with contempt.

As we moved through the ballroom, the party was more and more off the hook. There was a stage with a podium and a microphone, and hovering behind and above was a screen projecting remade movie trailers with Eben playing the leading man. A DJ was spinning music, and kids were dancing on the stage and on the floor. There were eight raised banquettes, and on top of each a professional dancer wearing Oscar's color: gold. There were four open sushi bars with sushi chefs rolling every imaginable combination. Huge posters of Oscar attendees Reese Witherspoon, Hilary Swank, and Keira Knightley were suspended from the ceiling like chandeliers. There was also a photo processing area that let you put your picture on any tabloid magazine cover you wanted: *Us, In Touch, Star, Life & Style.*

Arthur was getting annoyed and bored.

"Ladies, as riveting as your plight is, I'm waning. So if you don't mind, I will make myself scarce. Find me when you have achieved your puerile mission, and we can leave. In the meantime, because you've robbed me of at least four hours focusing on my life's work, I'll be lost in thought thinking about my patent." He spun on his heels, turned his back on us, and walked away.

We scanned the crowd and studied a couple of the teenage girls we didn't recognize. Some were loud and obnoxious, others had looks of utter disgust on their faces as they spotted someone's outfit they didn't like. One girl typed away on her Sidekick, another was fake smoking with an unlit cigarette.

These girls were massive divas in mini outfits. No one was going to be dancing the hora at this party.

And then we saw Kelly and The Chicas, lurking around, just outside the epicenter of the teens. They seemed to be imitating the other girls around them. Kym was staring at some tall Paris Hilton wannabe and copying her dance moves exactly, and Sara and Megan, in turn, were copying Kym's dance moves. Kelly was a terrible dancer, so no matter who she copied, it wouldn't have mattered. But she did seem pretty distracted, and perhaps even a bit overwhelmed by all the sophistication that was concentrated in this room.

"Remember, we have to out-cool The Chicas. When we have them where we want them, we'll tear off our wigs and reveal that the two NYC girls they thought were so awesome are really us. Then they'll be begging us to forgive them."

"I feel like I don't even know what's cool or not anymore," Lydia lamented. "This is all so out of my realm."

"We'll act like they act." I turned to her. "But just a little bit *more*.

"Sarah Jessica Simpson?"

"Yes, Winnie Foster?"

I looked her in the eye. "We have to be bitches."

Lydia's eyes widened with pleasure. We clasped hands and headed toward the dance floor, near Kelly and The Chicas.

My palms were dripping wet. I felt tiny tremors quake through my body as we approached them. We couldn't be found out so early. It would ruin everything. *Please don't recognize us. Please don't recognize us.* But there was no flash of recognition in their eyes. I exhaled with relief. We started to dance next to them.

They all looked great. Kym was decked out in a DKNY silver-foil eyelet spaghetti-strap dress. I had wanted that dress so badly, but my mother wouldn't even let me touch the picture in the catalog, it was so expensive. Her hair was down and her purse was on the ground next to her feet. Megan was in a brown jersey tube dress that gathered at the waist, and Sara was in a saddle-colored tank dress that had a wide ribbed waistband. Kelly's outfit was stunning. She was wearing a silk floral dress with five bands of lace and ruffles. It was gorgeous.

When I looked up, I realized that I wasn't the only one who was staring.

"Great outfits," Kym called from her spot on the dance floor. "Where'd you get them?"

"Oh, thanks," we said, altering our voices somewhat, working the disguise even more.

"Just a little boutique near our penthouse," I said. "We're from NYC."

"Wow. Really? You guys are so lucky. NYC is so exciting. Nothing ever happens in Rye. They should just change its name to Boring."

"Yeah, it seems really boring. We were going to drive and just like, you know, tool around this town, but we heard it was so dull, we didn't bother."

"Drive? You guys know how to drive?" Sara asked us.

"Yeah. What? You guys can't drive?" I asked.

They looked at each other.

"Well, sure. I mean, we know how to drive," Kym lied.

"That's a relief. Wouldn't want the town *and* the kids to be boring!" I said.

"Yeah," Lydia added.

The girls all stared at each other with wonder in their eyes. I could see what each of them was thinking. *Do you think I'm boring?* That's what Kym's face was asking Megan and that's what Sara's face was asking Kelly.

I stopped dancing and rolled my eyes.

"I'm gonna go get a drink and ask the DJ to put on some real music."

"Yeah. Some real music," Lydia echoed. The two of us

walked away toward the punch bowl. We wanted to shriek with excitement.

"They think we are so awesome," Lydia said.

"I know, I know. I can't believe this is actually working."

A couple of minutes later, Kym, Kelly, and The Chicas joined us at the punch table.

"You're right, this music is so not clubby," Kym said.

"Yeah, holler. It's so lame," Kelly said. Holler? Now she was using Kym-speak?

"Doesn't matter. We're gonna cut out of here early, anyway. Michelle Williams and Heath Ledger are having a party in Brooklyn and we were invited. We might go check it out," I said.

"If we're in the mood. You know, for Brooklyn," Lydia added.

"How did you get invited to that?" Kym asked, wide-eyed.

"What? You didn't hear about it?"

Kym shook her head no ever so slightly.

"Strange. I thought the party was really well publicized, but I guess not."

"Yeah. I guess not," Lydia said.

"Who else do you know?" Kym asked while Kelly, Megan, and Sara leaned in close.

I looked to the far end of the room, trying to think of someone else fabulous we could know. Eben was on the dance floor, dancing a weird flogging dance all by himself. Then I saw Arthur in a heated conversation with the photographer who resembled Louis Braille. They were both waving their arms furiously. Probably debating when air was invented or something.

"I really don't want to name-drop," I said.

"Yeah, we feel that that's really tacky."

"We won't tell," Kym pleaded.

"Okay, well if you must know. Gwyneth Paltrow was my babysitter when I was young and we developed a really close bond, so she's still in my life. So I have dinner with her and Chris, Apple, and Moses, like, I don't know, once a week?"

"Yeah, and Sarah Jessica Parker was my neighbor and that's who my parents named me after."

"Why would they name you after your neighbor?" Sara asked.

"Because when Sarah married Matthew they moved away and my parents missed her. So *voilà*! Anyone here speak French?"

The girls shook their heads no.

"*C'est la vie*," I said.

Oliver was heading our way. Kym saw me looking over her shoulder and she followed my gaze. He joined our circle. Arthur and the photographer were walking toward the DJ booth.

"Oh, I just LOVE this song," Kym said, louder than necessary. "Oliver, do you wanna dance with me?" she asked, raising her arms and shaking her hips in an effort to appear sexy.

"No, thanks," Oliver said and then grinned at me.

"Winnie, come check out the tabloid photo table. There's some hilarious stuff you have to see," he said, "great material for your act."

As I followed him, I heard Kym asking Lydia, "Her act? Is she on Broadway or something?"

Lydia caught up with us, and we all walked over to the tabloid station, passing by Eben along the way. I hid my face behind my curls and watched as Eben screamed at his parents until his cheeks were red.

His mother clasped a *Fiddler on the Roof* menorah and was near tears. Eben had his arms filled with tchotchkes: a Cave of Machpelah Tzedakah box and a bar mitzvah snow globe. He shoved them into his mother's arms and gestured with his hand for her to get rid of it all. His father finally grabbed the Judaica from Eben and said something in a low and harsh tone;

then Eben turned his back on his parents, while a small coterie of boys waiting in the wings rejoined him as he walked away. His parents looked at each other, frustrated, but worn down.

I guess he didn't want the Judaica to be so obvious or something, but he was acting really spoiled. If Rabbi Sherwin had been here, he would have leaned over and said out of the side of his mouth, *This here, Stacy, is a lot of* bar *but not a lot of* mitzvah. Eben hadn't changed one bit since the last time we saw him. I thought at least his bar mitzvah might have softened him; that he might have taken something from his Torah portion to heart, like I had with mine. I felt bad for his rabbi, for his temple, and especially his parents.

Lydia had caught Eben's tantrum too. I squeezed her hand and she squeezed back. We may have been doing something now that was not such an act of God, but at least we had respect for our heritage.

15. SCANDAL—CLIQUE CONSPIRACY!

Oliver and I got photos taken for the tabloid covers while Lydia ran to the bathroom to check her wig. Oliver and I were laughing so hard we had to hold each other up. We put our faces side by side and grinned. Our caption was so clever: WINN-IVER BABY CRISIS! We got two copies and kept one each.

When Lydia returned, I mean, Sarah Jessica Simpson, we all went to the dance floor. Arthur was now in the DJ booth with a pair of headphones on. His blue head was rocking out to the tunes, and every now and then he'd turn and he'd give the DJ the thumbs-up. I felt relieved that he wasn't making a stink or getting us caught by doing something embarrassing.

I thought that playing it a bit aloof was the way to go, so we purposefully excluded Kelly and The Chicas by taking Oliver to the dance floor.

"Great outfit," some girl called to me. "Is that Marc Jacobs?"

Sooner than I knew, Kelly and The Chicas were standing right near us, trying to dance their way into our little circle.

This was amazing. They were coming to us! I hadn't even imagined how well this might work. I smiled at Lydia.

Eben danced his way over, so Lydia and I spun and turned our backs to him. "Did I NOT tell you that this would be the best bar mitzvah in his-to-ry?" he bragged. We all said yes and then he grabbed Kym around the wrist, and not so subtly, planted her in the space between me and Oliver. "You guys should dance together. Seriously," Eben said, with a stern eye on Oliver.

Oliver smiled politely and Kym shook her hips wildly. *Très* rude. Then Eben danced away to be the center of attention elsewhere. Lydia and I spun back around.

"So you guys came all the way out here for this party?" Megan asked us.

"Yeah. We heard it was gonna be off the hook," I said, keeping my eye on Kym and Oliver. Oliver was eyeing me, helpless, like he was asking me to save him. I relished the moment.

"And your parents just let you come?" Sara asked.

"Um, yeah. You can do anything you want in New York City," I answered, trying to sound perfectly snotty.

"That is so cool," Kym said, turning to me. "I love your Chanel earrings, by the way. I wish my mother cool enough to let me wear earrings like that."

"Let me see," Oliver said, dancing his way back to me and away from Kym. He bent down to examine my earrings and I felt his warm breath in my face. His lips were at my cheek. It was all I could do to stop shaking.

"Very nice," he said.

This was a conundrum. I felt simultaneously powerful and cowardly. Kelly and The Chicas were throwing themselves at us, practically begging us to be friends. And then there was Oliver, who seemed to genuinely like me. Or me as Winnie, anyway.

"I spent the day in NYC this summer," Kelly said. "My dad took me to see *The Lion King*."

"We don't do Broadway. That's for tourists. Anyway, we were in Greece."

"My family has a house there," Lydia added.

I laughed. "A house? A house? That's no house, Sarah Jessica." Lydia looked confused and almost scared, as if I was turning on her. "Mansion is more like it," I said with a big white smile.

Lydia breathed a small sigh of relief. "Well, I don't want to brag."

"I've never been to Greece. I've always wanted to go," Oliver said.

"Maybe we'll take you," Lydia offered. "Every summer my parents let me choose a couple of friends to take and we bring them. All expenses paid by us. You'll even get your very own maid."

"My family has a house in Palm Beach," Kym said to Oliver.

"Yeah, so does my grandmother," Oliver said. "It's like a living cemetery down there."

We both laughed. Kym furrowed her brow.

"So what are the kids like here in Rye?" I asked them.

"Oh, they're okay. Nothing too special," Megan said.

"Yeah. I mean outside of us, there's no one that's really so cool," Sara offered.

"Yeah, we're the only cool girls in our class," Kym said. "Like you know, we're the clique."

Excuse me? The only cool girls?

I waited for Kelly to jump to her friends', Stacy and Lydia's, defense.

"There are no other cool girls in your class?" I asked, twirling a curl around my finger.

"There are these other two girls . . ." Kelly stammered.

"But they weren't cool enough to get invited!" Kym said, cutting her off with a cackle.

I eyed Lydia. Now was the time. We both reached our

hands up toward our wigs in order to rip them off in unison and yell, "SURPRISE!" but before we could, Kym raised her hand up to her own head and said, "Exactly!"

We had no idea what she was doing, so I pretended to have an itch on my head while Lydia stopped at her neck and pretended her tag was bothering her. Kym's hand then formed the shape of an L and rested now on her forehead, palm out, facing us.

"They are la-la-la-la-looooosers," she said.

Everyone laughed, and Megan and Sara followed, holding their L-shaped hands against their foreheads. They looked at Kelly. But she didn't follow them.

"Come on, Kelly. Or are you a la-la-la-la-Loser, too?" Kym said viciously. Very slowly, Kelly put her hands into the Loser L and held it up to her forehead.

I swallowed hard and Lydia looked like she was about to burst into tears.

STACY FRIEDMAN'S REMINDER TO SELF: You are not Stacy Friedman right now, you are Winnie Foster, so do not cry, DO NOT CRY.

"Oh, my God that is so LOL," I said, nearly choking on the words.

"So LOL," Lydia followed glumly.

Kym looked at us kind of funny.

"I'm thirsty," Oliver said, turning toward me. "You want to get more soda?"

"Sure," I said. He grabbed my hand and pulled me toward the soda fountain, dissing Kym in front of everyone. I turned back to catch Lydia's eye, but what I saw instead was Kym glaring at the two of us. Then she turned and stomped in Eben's direction. I glanced over toward the DJ booth and noticed Arthur wasn't there anymore. And Lydia was suddenly engulfed into the ether of the dance floor.

While we were getting a Coke, Oliver said, "Something's happening."

I almost said, "Between us?" but thankfully, I didn't. Because I realized he was definitely talking about something else, as clapping rose off the dance floor and a lone voice sang out single cheers.

"Opa!"

And then the entire dance floor called back,

"OPA!"

We walked a little closer, trying to make our way through the crowd, until we saw that the person leading the cheer was none other than Arthur Friedman himself. All the boys were still lined up against the wall, but not Arthur. After all, what did he have to lose? He didn't know these people. He didn't care about knowing these people. And he definitely loved to dance.

He was encased within a circle of girls. There must have been twenty around him, and he was doing hip-hop moves in the center. Each time he'd stand he'd call "OPA!" and the girls and the crowd would respond back, "OPA!" Soon Arthur's cheers were drowned out by the cheers of the girls. "Arthur! Arthur!" It sounded like we were at Madison Square Garden. Out of my peripheral vision, some flailing caught my eye. It was Kym and she was yelling at Eben, gesticulating wildly. Then they both turned to glare in my direction.

Uh-oh.

A voice from behind me said, "Your brother is one amazing dancer." I turned my head and found Oliver hovering right next to me. I broke out in a cold sweat, like I had cholera or the flesh-eating disease or something.

Kym and Eben started walking in our direction. Kym stuck out her chin all proud, while Eben seethed. They were like the junior high Mafia.

I tried to be as nonchalant as possible. I had to get out of here. "Will you excuse me for a second? Bathroom," I said quickly, to Oliver.

"Sure. I'll be here."

I ducked behind someone, and dodged out of the line of fire. I had to find Lydia. Our brilliant crashing plan was crashing and burning! We had to get out of here before we were confronted.

I didn't know where Lydia was, and I wasn't sure how we were going to discreetly grab Arthur when he was in the center of a cheering mob. I checked around to see if Eben and Kym were waiting to properly dispose of me, but I had lost sight of them.

"There you are."

I whirled around. Oliver, leaning casually against a banquet table. What was I supposed to do? I needed to get out of here, and now Oliver was standing next to me. I had to come up with some excuse.

"You know, I think that Sarah Jessica and I should really be going. We're gonna miss our train."

"Oh," he said, disappointed. "When is the train?"

"Like now," I said, slightly panicked.

"Oh," he said again. "Well, if you have to leave, then maybe we can exchange e-mail addresses or something."

"Uh . . . sure." liar@pantsonfire.com?

"Or we could exchange this . . ." he said and leaned down

toward my mouth. His face started to come toward mine until it went double and instead of one pair of lips puckering and closing in on mine, I saw two. He put his hands on my cheeks. I couldn't believe it: WE WERE GOING TO KISS! The fluttering butterflies in my stomach wafted away any fears I had, because his lips were a mere breath from touching mine!

But then a guttural scream froze us, and everyone else at Eben's bar mitzvah.

"CRASHER!"

Oliver dropped his hands from my face and looked around, confused, as to why the entire party was staring at us. The crowd parted like the Red Sea as Eben, Kelly, Kym, a party planner, and The Chicas strode right toward us.

Lydia quickly darted through the crowd, grabbed my hand, and stood by my side. When Kym reached me, she stared right into my eyes and said, "That is so LOL? That is SO LOL?"

Then her hand was on my head, and my wig was yanked off. Four small metallic clinks splattered to the floor. It was the sound of the bobby pins that had held the wig in place. Then a draft of cool air ran through my real hair. She was holding up my blond wig in her hand, shaking it as evidence, and exposing me for the fraud I was. The entire room gasped in unison.

"It's STACY FRIEDMAN!!" Kym yelled.

I felt out-of-body detached, so overwhelmed and frightened for the unraveling of my life. This was not the reveal Lydia and I had planned for. This was an unmasking. Arthur stood behind Kym. His hand was over his mouth, and his eyes bulged. I had never seen Arthur look as if he had no answers.

Kym was glaring at me, the venom practically oozing from her snaky tongue. She said in a low, mean whisper, "This is so *NOT LOL.*"

16. Nominated out the Door

Kym reached out and pulled Lydia's wig off her as well.

"And LYDIA KATZ!" Megan called out. The Chicas surrounded us in a semicircle.

"Oh, my God, you guys are such losers," Kym said. "Who still plays dress-up at this age?" Kym asked the teeming crowd.

With my wig off, my hair was flat and plastered to my head. I didn't even want to imagine what I looked like.

Eben wagged a finger in our faces. "How much did you guys eat? It cost my family three hundred dollars a head, so you better start writing down what you ate and pay us back."

As much as it pained me, I had to see what Kelly's reaction to all this was. Her arms were crossed and she was shaking her head, no. Her cheeks were red with embarrassment.

"Kelly," I said quietly. "I'm sorry."

"You made me look like a fool, pretending to be someone else," she hissed.

"We didn't mean it. We had good intentions. I can explain."

"I don't want to hear it," Kelly said.

I couldn't believe it. This was not the plan. This was not the way Lydia and I had envisioned this going.

Oliver's face seemed to have drained of all his blood. He looked horrified, confused, upset. "You tricked me?"

"No, I didn't . . . we didn't mean to . . ."

"You tricked me," he repeated. Only this time as a statement. His eyebrows were raised high, like we were a joke he didn't quite get. Oliver backed away from us.

"She's so not worth it, Ollie. You know she already has a boyfriend," Kym snarked as she sidled up to him and slipped her arm through his.

Oliver winced once again, and in a seeming state of shock, let Kym guide him over to The Chicas. I tried to meet Oliver's eyes, to apologize through expression, but he wouldn't meet my eyes. He was staring down, playing with the end of his tie.

I wanted to explain everything, why we crashed, who we were, that I didn't have a boyfriend anymore, and that no one but Lydia knew, but I couldn't even find a way to regulate my breathing. So I just kept gasping for air.

A party planner with black cat-eye glasses stepped forward and stood next to Eben, who was still in my face. I was terrified and mortified. It was all I could do to pull the E necklace out from under my dress. Lydia did the same thing. Eben lunged forward and ripped them off our necks.

People were craning their necks to see what was going to happen next. The party planner took the necklace out of Eben's hand and inspected.

"This piece was commissioned for the event! They're fakes!" The cat-eyed party planner asked the crowd, "Does anyone know these girls?"

We looked at Kelly and the party planner followed our eyes. "You," she said, "are these girls friends of yours?"

It was so quiet I swear I heard the flecks of gold glitter from my necklace hit the floor. Everyone looked at Kelly with pinched faces, waiting to see which side she would come down on. She never looked at us. She just turned back to the party planner and shook her head very slowly, side to side.

"Is that a no?"

"Yes. That is a no," Kelly responded.

Pause.

NO??

The party planner spoke into her walkie-talkie, and within seconds two other party planners were at her side. They grabbed Lydia, Arthur, and me by the backs of our shirts and practically ran us to the front door of the building. I could hear the kids behind us starting to talk and chatter. I turned back to the crowd to see if maybe Kelly would change her mind, call out, "Wait," but she didn't, and what I saw instead was almost worse than her silence. Kym stood between Kelly and Oliver. Kym reached out to her right and took Kelly's hand in solidarity, and then she cocked her head to the left and leaned it on Oliver's shoulder.

I knew then that was it. I had lost them both. I had lost my best friend and my potential boyfriend to the same girl. The crowd was getting smaller and smaller as we got farther away. Before I knew what was happening, the door opened, and we were literally thrown outside.

Quel humiliation.

We sat on the front steps, in shock at what had just transpired. The tears were welling up, and I blinked hard to keep them in.

We were not going to survive eighth grade. Lydia was pale, as pale as I'd ever seen her. The rash she gets when she's embarrassed was spreading across her neck and chest.

"We're finished," she said.

And before I had a chance to verbalize it, Arthur asked the very question we were all afraid to ask.

"Say, how are we gonna get home?"

We were SO dead.

17. The Road to Ruin

My mother didn't say a word the whole ride home. She gripped the steering wheel so hard her joints were white. Her mouth stayed pinched and her body was rigid. Arthur switched stations on the radio until my mother finally smacked his hand away, turning it off completely.

"Silence," my mother said.

I couldn't believe what was happening. It all felt so surreal. We had tried and failed to be accepted by our old friend in her new group. We had listened to her call us losers, and then watched Kelly deny us as friends. We had tried and failed to crash a bar mitzvah. We tried and failed to be one of the cool girls. And in one bold move, we lost our best friend forever.

We'd forever be known as the losers who crashed a bar mitzvah; the two that were so desperate to be part of something, they had to fake it. Kelly would ignore us when she saw us in public. She'd cross the street to the other side, avoid us in bathroom lines at the movie theater. When I flipped through the SLK photo album, it would feel like history. It would BE history. Honestly, I wanted to vomit. That's how sick I felt. Maybe I could convince Dante to take me back. Maybe I could move to Italy and live with him and his family, start all over again on foreign soil. How hard could it be to learn Italian? I already knew a few sentences. *Gradirei la pasta con la salsa della carne, ma prego non la cucinare in burro. Sono allergico alla latteria.* (I would like the pasta with meat sauce, but please don't cook it in butter. I am allergic to dairy.)

I unrolled the window and let some air come in. I watched the trees skim green past my face. The farther we got from the synagogue, the farther away Kelly felt.

Okay, God, I'm going to admit it.

I understand that what we did was wrong, crashing a party we weren't invited to, making necklaces to look like the real invites, but we were doing it all for the right reasons. Don't you understand?

See, I know that you were never a young girl so you may not know exactly how these things work, but when you're my age and you have best friends, the last thing you want is for one of those best friends to defect over to another side and get, like, new and improved best friends. The

Chicas, God, are like, the most popular girls in school and like, we were all just so fine and happy the way it was before, when it was the three of us and the three of them, and we started to sort of merge. But this is not a merge, this is a theft. They've stolen one of our members and turned her against us. They are brainwashing Kelly! And all we were trying to do here, God, was save her.

Mom dropped Lydia off, and when we got inside the house, she slammed the front door behind her.

"Stacy, I am *very* disappointed in you."

"Mom, don't make such a big deal out of it," I said in my best nothing-can-hurt-me voice. What was wrong with me? Why was I being so bitchy to my own mother?

"And since when are you allowed to wear makeup?"

"Whatever, chill. Holler."

"Excuse me?" My mom whipped around to face me. "I have no idea what's going on with you, Stacy. You lie to me, you crash a bar mitzvah." She started flailing her arms. "You're wearing an outfit I've never even seen before. I not only don't recognize you, I don't like this person very much."

I turned around and headed upstairs toward my room. I had one friend left. Lydia was all I had. And we had to return to school. We had to face the rest of the kids. How was I going to walk down the halls at school after the bar mitzvah fiasco? How was I possibly going to face The Chicas? Or Kelly? I could barely even process that Kelly had denied knowing me and Lydia. I mean, I had a lot of problems here, and now my own mother didn't even like me?

When I reached the top of the stairs, I realized my mother wasn't done. She was right behind me.

"I was with Alan and I had to leave and come get you. I had to cancel my trip in the middle of it because of you."

Without facing her, I answered, "I'm sorry."

"You'd better be sorry, young lady." My mother threw her purse down on the couch and went off to listen to the messages. Alan's was the first message and it made me feel awful.

"Hi, Shelley, so I guess that didn't work out. Sorry you had to leave before the sunset. I certainly hope it wasn't anything I said. Well, if you feel like giving me a call back, please do. Bye, now."

I started walking down the hall to my bedroom. I didn't like the tone of Alan's message. Why was he taking it so personally? My mom's bailing had nothing to do with him. It had to do with me. Didn't I have enough to worry about without having to add this to the list?

I closed the curtains and lay down on my bed and stared at the glow-in-the-dark stars and the time projected on my ceiling. It was only 4 p.m. Way too early to be home from a party already. In the darkness of my room, the stars just looked yellowish-green, nothing glowing or magical about them. Was that how Kym was? At school she was magical and powerful, but at home was she was just a normal kid? And what about Kelly? Did Kelly really think we were losers now? Did she really not want to be our friend because she just preferred Kym and The Chicas to me and Lydia? Or maybe what we had done was truly bad. I guess in some ways, I couldn't blame her for being mad. And what about Oliver?

I was up against some big obstacles. Maybe the stars were out of alignment, or Mercury was in retrograde or something. Maybe I could ride this out a few days and everything would just heal itself. I rolled over, exasperated.

Ugh. So, what? I was supposed to wait now for the stars to realign? That might take weeks, months! I couldn't ride this out for that long.

Now that I wasn't Winnie Foster and I wasn't popular, I had no idea what was left of the old Stacy.

18. Off the Hook

I woke up to the sound of the phone ringing. I forced myself back to sleep but was reawakened by three more phone calls. I remember, in between my fits of sleep, having some conscious realization that all wasn't lost after all. If the phone was ringing, I still had friends. My chest expanded with a slight feeling of hope. I rolled out of bed and my stomach immediately knotted as I stepped over my newly bought embroidered medallion dress. The most expensive dress I'd probably ever buy lay wrinkled in a ball on the floor. As I opened my door and smelled the eggs scrambling, my mother yelled,

"ARTHUR! It's the phone for you, again!"

Arthur? Getting phone calls? Did I wake up in the future? Was it the year 2030?

"Take a message, please!" Arthur called to her.

I ran down the stairs and sat down at the breakfast table. My mother put scrambled eggs on my plate and poured me orange juice, but didn't say good morning. I was afraid to say good morning to her. What if she didn't respond?

Arthur ran down the stairs and slammed himself into a chair. "These girls. They won't stop," he complained.

"What are you talking about?" I asked.

"They're texting me like crazy!" he shrieked as he thrust his phone into my face. Sure enough there were eleven messages waiting in the inbox. "And the phone, it's ringing off the hook."

"For you?" I asked, incredulous.

"Yes, for me, who else?"

A brief flood of anxiety washed through me.

"Well, what do they want?" I asked.

"They want to LOVE me!" he screamed, horrified.

"Why would they want to love you?" I asked, genuinely confused. "Sorry. That came out wrong. What I meant was, why do they want to love you?"

"Because apparently, I'm fabulous!" he yelled, completely unnerved by this idea. "None of the other boys were dancing. They were all lined up against the wall, texting each other and not asking anyone to dance. I was the only boy my age who danced. Have you seen my moves? I'm spectacular!"

His phone vibrated again. The real phone rang again. I raced to get it.

"Hello?"

A young girl's voice quivered when she asked, "Hi, um, does Arthur Friedman live here?"

"Yes," I said tersely.

The girl then covered the mouthpiece with her hand and whispered to her friends, "He does live there!" And then I heard a chorus of giggles.

"Can I talk to him please?"

Arthur was shaking his head a vigorous no, and making a slashing motion across his neck.

"He is indisposed at the moment."

"Um . . . what?"

I rolled my eyes. "He's busy. Can I take a message?"

"Um . . . okay. Can you tell him that Eliza called?"

"Sure. Does he have your number?"

"Um . . . I don't think so, but never mind. I'll just e-mail him."

"Okay. Whatever you say."

I hung up and sat back down next to Arthur. "This is unbelievable. You're a hero for doing the same thing that's going to make me a pariah."

"Quite the paradox, isn't it?" Arthur asked as he poked around at his breakfast without taking a bite.

"If you ladies will excuse me," Arthur said, and ran up to his room.

My mother sat down in Arthur's empty seat.

"I'd like to know how you got the money to buy such an expensive dress."

I looked at my feet.

"I'm waiting," my mother said, drumming her fingers on the counter top.

"I used my bat mitzvah money," I admitted, sheepishly.

I looked up at my mother's stunned face, and then I quickly turned away. I was waiting for her to start yelling at me, but all she did was say, in a monotone voice, "You're grounded."

"It doesn't matter," I said, snottily. "Because I have nowhere to go!"

"Good, then the time you spend at home should make you quite happy," she said before turning and walking out of the kitchen.

I didn't even have time to call after her, because suddenly there was an emergency from upstairs.

"STACY! I NEED YOU!" Arthur called from his room.

I ran upstairs to Arthur's room, where he was sitting in his swivel chair at his computer. "They're sending me friend invites to MySpace. I don't even have a MySpace page! You know my position about these online social sites. To relate to each other through an interconnected system of networks that connects computers around the world via the TCP/IP protocol is just asking too much of me. Despite the fact I'm building a robot in order to clean my room, at heart I'm really a Luddite. Stacy, my sense of moral decency is being severely compromised here."

I shook my head. This kid was too much.

"Move over."

I kneeled in front of his computer, and sure enough his e-mail account was filling up with MySpace invites. The IMs were chiming in faster than anyone would have been able to respond. The phone rang again. Arthur picked it up and hung it up.

I typed "Arthur Friedman" into the friend-finder search field. Lo and behold, Arthur's name popped up, and I clicked the link.

"Oh, my God," I said, shocked. An audio stream popped up and began to play a clip. At first, it just sounded like kids screaming until a singular voice called out, methodically, rhythmically, "OPA! OPA!" A photo of Arthur was wallpapered over the site, probably lifted off the robot-building online community.

He was wearing a suit and tie and was proudly holding a small Styrofoam model of his room-cleaning robot.

Arthur swiveled back to me in his chair. "How did this happen?"

"They must have made you a page," I said.

"Is that legal?"

"I guess so."

The bottom of the page was filled with comments from girls from Eben's middle school.

"I OPA to see you soon!" a pretty blonde girl who went by the handle "Sillisally" wrote.

"Rock-starTHUR!" another girl, Valerylovesyou, wrote.

"I don't even know these people. They don't even know me, how could they possibly know what they like, when they don't even know who I am!"

"Welcome to celebrity, Arthur."

"I might have to dye my hair!" he exclaimed. "Go into the Witness Protection Program."

I considered this. "You know, that's actually not a bad idea. Do you think mom would go for it? I mean we wouldn't be able to see Dad or Delilah again, but we could go anywhere, change our names, our hair, everything."

"I think one can only join the program if their life is in jeopardy, not when they're suffering from an overabundance of affection."

Another MySpace invite appeared, and suddenly, I got an idea. I went back to the friend finder and typed in the name Oliver Solomon. Sure enough his MySpace page came up. There was a link to send a message, but I didn't want to do that in front of Arthur, so I quit out and headed to my room.

"You didn't help me!" Arthur yelled after me.

"Just start packing," I called back.

I had to explain myself to Oliver and I had to get him to forgive me. This was going to be rough. Finally, when I had gathered the courage, I sat down and composed what I thought was a pretty solid message. I went back to his MySpace page, clicked "send message," and typed away.

Dear Oliver,

This is Stacy Friedman (aka Winnie Foster). I'm sorry that I told you my name was Winnie Foster when it's really Stacy Friedman, as you now know. I'm sorry I lied to you about my name, but my friend and I really wanted to come to the bar mitzvah, and the only way we could go was if we crashed. Anyway, I'm sorry. Now you know my real name. And I also don't have a boyfriend. We broke up in the summertime. And I also don't live in New York City. I live in Westchester.

Sincerely,

Stacy Adelaide Friedman

I pressed SEND and sat and waited for a reply. I stared at my e-mail account. I refreshed. I refreshed again. I was refreshing myself into a frenzy, so it was a good thing that I was interrupted with a scream from Arthur.

"STACY!!"

I went running to his room.

"What is it?" I asked, concerned.

"They started a blog on my MySpace page! They are writing about me!" I shoved him out of the way and read the first post, whose title was "The Antics of Arthur."

This blog is dedicated to Arthur Friedman and his antics. This weekend Arthur crashed a bar mitzvah that got him kicked out! But while he was there, he busted the dopest moves in town. We've never seen any boy dance so well—we've never really seen any other boy dance! Arthur wore a Ramones

shirt, ripped-up pants, Puma sneakers and
blue hair. What will he do next? Stay tuned.
We will be blogging regularly about Arthur,
the Rock Starthur's local stunts. We are:
Eliza, Ruby, Mila, and Camille, but just
call us The Arthurettes!

"Oh, my God, Arthur. They're like stalkers. They're going to blog your every move. What are you gonna do?"

"What if the robot community gets wind of this? How in the world will I be taken seriously by my colleagues, especially if I can't get Hudi to work? I'll have you know I'm no huckster. I'm not interested in stunts, ploys, pranks, or gags of any nature. I am not a man of antics. I am Arthur Friedman. Scientist. Engineer. Ph.D. candidate."

"Maybe you should write the robot community a letter and explain things. That might help," I said, thinking really of myself and the letter I had just sent Oliver.

"No. I'm gonna take this to the top."

"Mom?" I asked.

"No, higher. I'm going straight to the principal's office tomorrow."

I went back to my computer to see if Oliver had e-mailed

me back, but he hadn't. I was starting to realize that the boy I lied to was a boy I had genuine feelings for. I sat at my desk and then was hit by an even better idea. I typed in Kelly's name and up came her page. I clicked on it, but then a message alert appeared. It said, "Friends Only." Even though I saw the words, I couldn't quite believe what I was seeing. Friends only. What was I? An enemy?

19. Don't Marni Gross Me!

Hi, God,

Okay, I admit it. I'm terrified. I'm terrified of returning to school tomorrow.

For the sake of the argument, let's say, hypothetically speaking, my mother actually let me throw a party, and let's say that at said fictional party, Marni Gross just happened to come when I SO clearly hadn't invited her. No problem. I'd suck it up. Who cares? Big deal! C'est La Vie. Live and learn. Roll with the punches.

Okay, I'd totally care. Marni Gross washes her hair with soap, which is disgusting. Lydia and I, however, do not wash our hair with soap.

I thought crashing was the right thing to do at the time. Okay, so maybe I didn't really think it through. I didn't consider the consequences, and maybe things spiraled a bit out of control and we pretended to know famous people, vacation in Greece, and speak French. It was dumb. I get it. I'm sorry. If given the opportunity I wouldn't do it again. Or at least I would do it differently.

Last year everyone accepted me, but this year I feel like I'm the same and they don't. So what do I do? How do I act? What should I wear? I'm really at a loss here, God. I need your help. I know that you can't dress me, but the least you could do is salvage my reputation.

Please help me, God. Please help me and Lydia understand what it is we're supposed to do; or how it is we're supposed to behave now. Because honestly, we just don't know anymore. Every step becomes a misstep. Every effort backfires on us. Whatever happens, I beg of you, please do not make us losers. Do not Marni Gross us.

With all due respect,
Stacy Adelaide Friedman

20. Worst-Case Scenario

Lydia and I met near the faculty entrance where none of the kids would see us. We were nearly catatonic with fear, absolutely terrified of facing Kelly and The Chicas and discovering what our newfound status was.

"On a scale of one to scared, how freaked out are you?" Lydia asked.

"Terrified," I answered. "You?"

"Petrified."

We could see kids running up the steps into school from where we stood. When the last kid ran in, it was time to go. The bell was going to ring and we'd be late, getting us into further trouble. What was next for us, Sing Sing?

"Are you ready?" I asked her.

"Not really," she answered. "Are you?"

"Never been less," I said. "You know what they say—" I started. Lydia looked at me. No, apparently, she didn't know what they said. "Wherever you go . . . there you are."

Lydia stared at me, expressionless.

"Sorry," I said. "I didn't mean to be punny."

Lydia cocked her head, annoyed. Not the right time for jokes, I guess.

We trudged through the faculty entrance, up through the faculty staircase, and emerged on our floor. With our heads held high, we walked down the hall. No one really turned to gawk at us, which was a good sign. Maybe this wasn't a big deal after all.

When we reached our floor, we saw The Chicas and Kelly, laughing and hanging around the lockers. Kym was demonstrating the dance move, the running man, and Kelly was braiding Megan's hair while Sara braided Kelly's. We had to walk by them to get to our lockers. I started trembling and sweating a little bit. I felt like one of those little short-haired dogs who shake all the time. As we neared them, Kelly spotted us, but turned her head away before even saying hello. The rest of The Chicas saw us too, and as we walked past, we were unsure whether we should pretend we didn't do anything wrong, but then The Chicas started to giggle. And then Kym coughed into her hand while simultaneously saying, "crashers." Then they all did it. Everyone in the little huddle was coughing into their hands while saying "crashers." Even Kelly. It was horrible. Like getting Avian flu. Only worse.

We took that as a sign to keep on walking.

In art, Kara and Nina were sitting next to each other and were talking loudly enough for all to hear.

"Are you going to Kelly's on Friday?"

"Duh. Everyone who's anyone will be there."

Friday night! That was when we were supposed to have our next sleepover. And at Kelly's!

"That Evite that they sent this weekend was so cool."

"Oh, I know, and I loved the funny thing that Kelly added at the bottom, about the bring your own lips."

"Kelly is so cool."

They had sent an e-mail invitation over the weekend? Neither Lydia nor I received one, which could only mean one thing. We were not invited. Again.

And what was this whole "bring your own lips" thing? What was funny about that? So now Kelly was renouncing our weekly sleepovers and replacing them with parties we weren't even invited to?

In homeroom Lydia and I sat together. The Chicas and Kelly were sitting in the corner being obnoxiously loud.

"Ohmygod you guys . . . Pause. Eben is like the best boyfriend ever," Kelly said. Lydia and I looked at each other. Boyfriend? Pause?

"See, what did I tell you?" Kym said.

"He like made his mom drive us to Stamford because the movie he wanted to see was playing only there. She like does whatever he says. Anyway, he bought me a rose. Holler."

"Ohmygod—jealous!" Kym squealed. "Saturday night double-dating? You and Eben, me and Oliver?"

I could barely stomach the rest of homeroom. Kym and Oliver sitting in a tree. I wanted to chop it down.

On my way downstairs to lunch, I passed by the ninth-grade homeroom. Two girls were inside the empty classroom gossiping and I stopped, caught off guard by something. I couldn't quite tell who they were, based on voices alone. Was it possible that people I didn't even know were gossiping about me?

Girl #1: They like just crashed, no invitation, nothing. They made fake invitations.

Girl #2: (*laughs*) That is so sad.

Girl #1: That's not even the worst of it.

Girl #2: What?

Girl #1: Stacy Friedman like, SO cheated on that kid Dante, remember, the exchange student from last year?

Girl #2: The supercute soccer player?

Girl #1: Yeah. She double-timed him with Eben's best friend. Gross, right?

Girl #2: Totally gross.

Girl #1: I'm so glad I'm not them.

Girl #2: Copy that.

I wanted to burst into the room and tell them I wasn't a cheater and I wasn't gross, but I was frozen, clutching my books to my chest.

People

Were

Gossiping

About

Me

And

Not

In

A

Good

Way.

At lunch, Lydia and I held a Friedman-Katz summit. I told her what I had overheard in the art room. Turns out this "everyone who is anyone" party was a make-out party hosted by Kelly and The Chicas. Kym had arranged it so that Kelly could kiss

Eben for the first time and so that—and here Lydia paused—
Oliver was going to kiss Kym for the first time. They were
both official couples now. And they were going to kiss. And
that made me want to hurl in a variety of colors.

How could Oliver have forgotten about me already? I know
that I had blown my big chance, but couldn't he mourn a little
more? Be a little more heartsick? Call in sick from school and
stay in bed all day? Shed some eye liquid? Why did he have to
move on so fast, and of all people, why with Kym?

Lydia and I were despondent, dejected. We couldn't eat our
food, which I guess wasn't the worst thing in the world.
Because it was Fish Stick Monday.

21. Tuck Is Not Everlasting

By the next morning, Lydia and I came up with a plan. It only took one day before we were tired of sitting alone at lunch, on the sidelines in gym, of being eyed by the Mathletes, the Cheerleaders, the Artists, the Jocks.

We decided to do something very adult. We were going to explain ourselves. With no lies, or exaggerations. We were going to be honest and heartfelt. Perhaps I'd throw in one perfectly timed joke to lighten the air, break the tension, but I never plan my improvisational moments in advance. The point is we were going to lay ourselves out there, expose our inner demons and flaws, and right all the wrong we had conjured.

During study hall in the library, we noticed Kelly was sitting alone, puzzling over her math homework. So, bravely, we headed over to her table. We stood at the head of her table with our books, and waited for her to look up. Which she didn't.

"Kelly?" I whispered.

"Can we talk to you?" Lydia asked quietly. Kelly searched the library as if she was anticipating company.

"I don't think that's a good idea," she said.

"Can't we just sit down for one minute?" I asked.

"Shhhh!" someone from a nearby study carrel said.

"Sorry!" I whispered back.

"Why don't you go sit where you belong, with the weirdos," a voice from behind us said. We turned and faced Kym. Standing on either side of her were Megan and Sara. They pushed past us and took their seats at the table.

"What's that supposed to mean?" Lydia asked.

"It means this is the cool table and you guys don't belong here," Sara said. Megan nodded in agreement.

"Do you think that too, Kelly?" Lydia asked.

Kelly didn't even look at us when she answered. "Well, what you guys did was really weird. I don't even know who you are anymore. It just seemed like, really desperate. So, umm, I guess Kym is right; it's probably not a good idea for the two of you to sit with us."

Lydia and I turned away and began walking. A tear fell from my eye and hit the cover of *Jane Eyre*.

"We're losers," Lydia said.

"Losers," I repeated, just to hear the word.

We sat down at an empty table, pulled out our books, and stared at the words in silence. We were so confused and so sad. I was afraid that if I opened my mouth to say anything, I'd just start bawling. I knew Lydia felt the same. I wished my school had an online attendance option, so I could pack up all my books and take classes from my bedroom computer. Suddenly, Lydia stood up, pushed her chair back and ran to the bathroom. I ran after her.

I leaned against the mirror and Lydia washed her hands.

"Is this how it's going to be now?" Lydia asked. "We're just gonna keep sinking lower and lower on the totem pole?"

There was a flush and then a stall unlocked, and out came Kelly. We stood shocked to see her and froze for a second, but she continued to the sink. No one said a word. She casually pulled some paper towels from the dispenser, as if she had all the time in the world. She crumpled the paper towel and threw it in the metal garbage bin and headed out toward the door. She seemed to hesitate as her arm reached for the handle, as if she might turn around and say something, but she didn't. Lydia and I waited, but Kelly just walked through the door and out to her new friends.

Lydia and I looked at each other, and then she burst into tears. I went over to comfort her, but when I put my arm around her, she shook it off, turned to me, and said, "It was your idea to crash that bar mitzvah."

"So this is my fault?"

"Well, it's not mine! I was friends with The Chicas last year, and now because of your dumb plan," Lydia said, tears trailing down her cheeks, her lower lip trembling and voice rising, "I can't even sit at the same table with them, and now Kelly thinks we're weird!"

"I was friends with The Chicas last year, too. And you went along with the crashing plan. You loved the idea!"

"Well, I refuse to be a loser and I certainly don't want to be known as a weirdo!" Lydia said as she began to make her way to leave. "I have half a mind to tell The Chicas this was all your idea in the first place!" she nearly shouted as she stormed off.

I stood there, in the bathroom, the weak overhead light giving an already depressing room a sickly coat of greenish light. Every last person in this building had friends. Even the kids in detention, the kids smacking erasers together to suck up to the teachers, had friends. I, on the other hand, suddenly had no one. I locked myself into a stall, bent over, and cried.

22. Friendless Friedman

I ran out of school literally as the last bell was ringing. I didn't want to see anyone and I didn't want to be seen. Since the bathroom incident, I had managed to keep my tears in for the rest of the day, but they were bursting at the seams, and I was desperate to get home where I could throw myself on my bed, and sob myself to sleep.

I stood at the bus stop, but then realized Lydia would be getting on the bus too. I just didn't know how to handle yet another confrontation, so I stepped out of line.

"Did you want me to save your place?" a quiet voice asked.

I turned around. Marni Gross, of all people, smiled at me.

"Um, I think I'm going to walk home," I said. "But thanks."

I called my mom because I'm not really supposed to be late without telling her. And she told me it was fine, but not to make any stops along the way. I was grounded, after all.

I watched my feet as I walked. I had never felt more alone. I passed the movie theater, and when I smelled the popcorn I decided to disobey my mom. It would take seven minutes at most. She'd never know. I would eat the popcorn on the way home. Maybe I'd buy some Jujyfruits, also. I was depressed. I wanted candy.

I ran into the theater and waited on line at the concession stand. A team of boys came in. They were rowdy and loud, like they were performing for an audience. Normally, I'd have turned around and maybe even glared at them, but I just didn't care today.

"I'm so macking on her. It's gonna be awesome. Doesn't she look like she'd be a good kisser?" a familiar-sounding boy asked his friends.

"Well, I wouldn't have kissed her last year, that's fer sure," a different boy added.

It was my turn at the concession stand. I asked for the candy and a small popcorn.

"What are you talking about?" the boy behind me asked his friend.

"I heard she used to be fat, man. Like a tire waist and blimpy thighs."

The concession guy rang me up, and I handed him a ten-dollar bill.

"Shut up. She was fat?" The kid was alarmed. "I don't want to make out with a former fat girl. What if some of her cellulite gets into my bloodstream?"

"Don't be an idiot," the other kid said. "Fat can't travel." And then he asked, "Can it?"

The concession guy put the change in my open palm and I put it in my pocket. As I turned, I saw Eben and his two follower friends, just as Eben was saying, "I'll make out with her at the party just for practice, but then I'm dumping her. There's seriously no way I'm dating a former chubbette."

I kept walking before they could recognize me, and when I got outside I was breathing really heavily, as if I had just eluded getting caught after a chase. I was dumbfounded and sickened by what I had just heard. Not just because it was hideously mean, but because it was about Kelly. Eben cared more about what Kelly used to look like than he cared about who Kelly even was.

I walked home the rest of the way completely confused by the events of eighth grade so far. Kelly was so different now. And while Eben saw her new self as good and her old self as bad, I felt the complete opposite. I didn't like the new Kelly at all.

STACY FRIEDMAN'S COMMENT ON LIFE: Anyone who says life is not hard never experienced eighth grade.

I went to my bedroom, sat on my bed, and ate my Jujyfruits, one after another. I didn't even wait to swallow a mouthful before shoving more in.

So this is what it looks like, God. This is what being friendless is: having no one to turn to; dreading the turning of the clock as it inches closer to the next day of school; mapping out areas, hallways, corridors, and stairwells where one can safely travel without smashing into The Chicas, who think you're a joke, into Kelly, who is embarrassed by you, and Lydia, who thinks you ruined her life. Even my house isn't a comfort zone. My own mother thinks I'm revolting. I don't know what Arthur thinks of me, but it's probably a word I've never heard of. All I have left is my bedroom. My only safe refuge. And the slight hope that Oliver wrote me back through MySpace.

Then, obsessive that I was, I checked my e-mail to see if Oliver had written back.

He had.

And it wasn't good.

> *Dear Stacy,*
>   *Sorry about you and your boyfriend. I'm going out with Kym now. She doesn't lie.*
>   *From,*
>   *Oliver*

Even though it was still light out, I climbed into my bed. I pulled back the covers and got underneath them fully clothed at six in the evening. During my main set on stage at the Stacy Friedman Pityfest, I heard giggling coming from Arthur's room. The giggling of girls. Could it be that Arthur had girls over?

I sat up. I got out of bed. I left my room, turned the corner and stood outside his slightly ajar door. I pushed it open a bit more and peeked in. Sure enough, there they were. Arthur was sitting on his bed, a book on string theory open on his lap. The music was blasting, and four girls were in the corner dancing.

"Come on, Arthur," one girl in the pack yelled, "make us laugh. Be funny!"

"Yeah, Arthur. Come on, you LOVE this song, remember?" another girl said

But Arthur just sat on the edge of his bed.

"Come on Arthur, dance!" one of the girls said.

"Yeah, entertain us. Be like you were at Eben's bar mitzvah!"

"OPA!" a girl called out and the remaining three responded in unison, "OPA!"

They all turned to Arthur—they had expectant, hopeful grins—but Arthur didn't look up. Instead, he walked over to Oman Hudi and started tinkering with the parts. He plugged the robot in and clapped, but the robot just stood there, lifeless. He put his hands on his hips and looked up to the sky, as if chastising God for not helping him with his grand, room-cleaning robot scheme.

A cute girl with straight honey-colored hair separated from the group and sat on the floor next to Arthur. She tried to get his attention by picking up some of the spare parts of Oman Hudi and pretending to really study them; but as anyone who knows Arthur knows, this is a lethal maneuver. Never EVER touch his engineering parts or tools without asking. Arthur was visibly annoyed (small red hives on the back of his neck, flared nostrils, and lips scrunched together).

"What is this going to be used for?" she asked, holding up what looked liked a metal bracelet.

"Not using it anymore," Arthur said, taking it out of her hand and placing it out of her reach.

"How are you going to make him move?"

"Not sure," he answered, not meeting her eyes.

"Will you have a remote control? Will it be solar or have a rechargeable battery source?"

"Don't know," Arthur said again.

Why was he being so monosyllabic?

"Arthur!" one girl whined. "You're not being any fun!"

Well, this is ironic, I thought. Here people were throwing

themselves at Arthur, vying for his attention and friendship, and he didn't want it, whereas I have been alone in my bedroom, desperate for my friends to fling themselves at me like this. *God, why is it that sometimes things just don't add up?*

Later that night, at dinner, the phones were remarkably quiet.

"Listen to that. Isn't the silence nice?" my mother asked. And just as she finished speaking, the phone rang, and we all jumped and then sort of awkwardly laughed without really connecting eyes.

My mother tossed down her napkin and excused herself from the table.

"Hello," my mother sang in her phone voice.

"No, Arthur is eating dinner now. Yes, I'll have him call you back."

My mother sat down.

"Those girls are so annoying. They're so demanding. How am I supposed to get any work done? I can't make my robot work, and they're clogging up my e-mail account with useless information. They just want me to be fun, fun, fun. I can't take it! I'm not fun! I'm very serious. But they don't care about serious Arthur."

"That one girl seemed to care. The one inspecting Oman Hudi," I said.

"Eliza?" he asked.

"I guess so." I shrugged. "She was asking you a bunch of questions."

"She was probably just being polite. Besides, I don't even know what to say to her."

"She was asking about your robot—how could you not know?"

"Well she's just the slow one of the bunch. As soon as she realizes I'm not fun, she'll stop asking me questions."

"That was her on the phone just now, so I don't think she's stopping yet," my mother said.

Arthur grimaced, turned bright red, and then hid his face in his hand. Arthur suffered from too much positive attention, and I suffered from none.

23. Rabbi Knows Best

A few days later, we dressed up for Kol Nidre, the Yom Kippur service at our synagogue. Because I was a bat mitzvah last year, I observed Yom Kippur the way my mother did and fasted the entire day. I had never really given much thought to the meaning of this holiday before, but Yom Kippur means "Day of Atonement," and it suddenly felt important to me. The day is set aside to atone for the sins of our past year—to make repentance and amends with God. Can you believe they give you just one day?

Arthur and I stayed home on Yom Kippur. We weren't allowed to watch television or make phone calls, eat, or drink. We were allowed to read, but only literature, not magazines, and my mother said we had to put aside one full hour where we did nothing but think about the past year. An hour was not enough time. I spent most of the day worried about what was happening at school without me. Maybe I was being unanimously voted out of my grade right this very minute. Maybe

Lydia was at home, blacking me out of her photo albums.

I loved Kol Nidre services. There was something about them that seemed more urgent than the others. But also, Rabbi Sherwin was the best rabbi in the world. He managed to make things interesting for everyone, even the hard of hearing. He could connect with everyone, just by telling a story.

Today he talked about Hilchot T'shuva, the laws of repentance. He said that everyone should make three honest attempts to reconnect. If the other person refuses, it's okay, because it's the attempt that counts. He talked about the ultimate Kol Nidre question: What's left undone? And he told us that we should try to right one wrong. He said that Kol Nidre is about promises and we should promise not to leave our lives undone.

And I swear he directed the whole sermon to me. He was watching where I was sitting almost the whole time. It was like, he just knew!

Afterward, my mother, Arthur and I went to thank him. He was glad to see us.

"Stacy, you look beautiful," he said. I blushed, of course. "Thank you, Rabbi Sherwin."

"And Arthur! Fit as an ox." Arthur beat on his chest like a monkey, which was funny because Rabbi Sherwin said ox, not monkey.

"And Shelley, a revelation."

"Oh, stop it, Rabbi. You're too kind."

"Just reporting the facts, ma'am."

We said our good-byes and as we headed down the aisle, I looked at my mother who was still angry with me for being crash-spastic and Arthur (who was crash-tastic but who didn't even know how to communicate with girls). I thought about Lydia, who wasn't speaking to me and the friends I no longer had. I stopped in my tracks, and something that Rabbi Sherwin said struck home with me.

"I'll be just a second," I said, and I turned around and fast-walked up to Rabbi Sherwin. He peered down at me as he shook the last person's hand.

"Rabbi Sherwin, do you have a minute?"

"Of course, Stacy. I have an unlimited calling plan for you," he said. I didn't really get that, but I smiled anyway.

He put one of his big hands on top of the other. "How can I help you?"

"Well, I just wanted to say thanks for the sermon."

"Ah, you liked it?"

I smiled shyly and nodded my head yes.

"It applied to you?"

I nodded my head yes again.

"It's difficult not to get lost and caught up in the surface of things, but if you can try and hold on to one thing, it should be to reconnect with the essence of who you truly are."

I put my hand up to my straight hair and touched it. It felt so different than my curly hair. This hair was simple, but my curly hair was complicated.

And I realized something. Just because other people don't like you, didn't mean you were unlikable.

I looked up at the stage, at the bema, where I had stood last year and spoke about sacrifice without really having practiced it. I couldn't very well complain about losing friendships when I hadn't done very much to practice being a good friend. Not this year, at least. Not when I had changed so much. For the worse.

I smiled at Rabbi Sherwin. I felt lighter than I had in weeks. I felt more confident, like I had purpose, because suddenly I did. I understood something now that I hadn't an hour ago.

I suddenly didn't care about being popular, I cared about something else much more. I cared about being a good friend and about doing the right thing. I cared about being a true person, true to me. Maybe Kelly didn't want to be my friend, anymore, but it didn't change the fact that I didn't want to see her get hurt.

Yes, I wanted to be included and I wanted to be popular, but more than that, I was realizing, I wanted to like who I was. And I knew that who I was, was a really good friend.

That evening, after the services, and after I had come to a very mature decision, inspired by Rabbi Sherwin's sermon, I knocked on my mother's door.

"Come in!" she called. She was lying on the couch, reading a self-help book, *How to Love Again without Being Hurt Again*.

"I thought you were going to dinner with Alan," I said.

"Well, I had to cancel it, Stacy. I can't exactly have Arthur babysit you, now can I?"

"Mom, I don't need a babysitter."

"Well, apparently you do. Whenever I leave you alone lately, something seems to go wrong."

"I promise I won't do anything wrong. I just want to go to Lydia's for a few hours. Please. You go out with Alan, and I'll be at Lydia's. You can call me on my cell phone every ten minutes if you want."

"I don't want to call you every ten minutes, Stacy. I want to be able to trust you. You crashed a bar mitzvah, you spent your bat mitzvah money on a dress to crash the bar mitzvah in. You made your brother an accomplice by asking him to fake the invitations. So no, you can't go to Lydia's. You will finish your chores, and much to my chagrin, I will remain here on this couch until you are finished."

I desperately needed to see Lydia. First, to make up with her and second, to tell her about my decision. I had to make my mother see the light. Otherwise, she was going to use everything I did wrong as an excuse not only not to trust me, but to avoid going out with Alan, whom I think truly made her happy. Because since this whole thing went down, Alan had been leaving her messages, and I knew by his voice that my mother was not returning them.

My mother and I sat facing each other on her bed. I had a couple of options. I could yell and scream and cry, throwing myself on the ground and begging her to let me go—and if we're to be honest—that was my impulse. Or, I could compose myself and tell her exactly why, in calm tones, punishing me was very bad idea. I counted to ten before I said anything. By the time I got to ten, the impulse to heave myself on the floor had all but disappeared.

"I understand what I did was really bad," I said.

"Good."

"And I've thought long and hard about what I've done. It's Yom Kippur; all I've done is atone for my sins. Not letting me go to Lydia's isn't going to make what I did sink in any more than it already has."

"Well, that might be so, but—"

"Okay. I'll confess. I was talking to Rabbi Sherwin at temple, and I realize that I haven't exactly been acting like myself lately. I've been rude and not who I am, and I'm really sorry. I am really going to try and be better."

My mother closed her book and put it down on her lap and turned toward me. She put her hand on mine and smiled.

"But," I added—and here she met my eyes and looked worried like I was going to pull the rug out from under her— "I think that Alan might be getting the wrong impression."

"What do you mean?" my mother asked, concerned.

"I think you might be sending mixed messages. You left in the middle of the canoe trip because of me and now, when you should be making it up to him, you're canceling."

My mother was unmoved by my argument.

"While it's an interesting theory, I'm not convinced. I'm staying home with you, tonight. I'm afraid I haven't been a very good mother myself these days. Too distracted, when you and your brother obviously need me."

"Dad and Delilah are living together now. It's okay for you to go on dates. Even to have a boyfriend. It's okay with me.

And I know it's okay with Arthur, too. Have you ever heard Arthur talk to anyone but us about his robot? No. But he talks to Alan about it. Unless, of course, you don't want to go on the date with Alan, and this is your sneaky way of getting out of it without being honest."

"One thing has nothing to do with the other, Stacy. You lied and now you're grounded. I can't help the timing of things. I would be going out with Alan tonight if I didn't have to babysit you."

"But you don't have to babysit me. That's what I'm trying to say." Then I took a deep breath and found it. My brain and my tongue connected and I turned to my mother and said, "Maybe this isn't about babysitting me, maybe, just maybe, it's about you and"—I glanced at her self-help book on her lap—"your fears of getting hurt again?"

She unconsciously crossed her hands over the book, covering the title. My mother opened her mouth, like she was about to argue back. But then she just sighed.

"Go on this date, Mom."

My mother folded her arms across her chest, assessing me, studying me to see if I was the real thing.

"You really surprise me, Stacy Friedman."

I smiled, proud.

24. Naturally, of Course

I jumped in the shower, washed my hair, and then jumped out. I towel dried, forgoing the blow-drying and straightening, and let it dry naturally. Then instead of the gauchos and Victorian inspired blouse favored by The Chicas, I put on the clothes favored by The Old Me. One pair of Stacy Friedman beat-up jeans and a soft, perfectly broken-in old camp T-shirt of Arthur's. I looked like myself. I felt like myself.

I yelled good-bye to my mother, who was in her bathroom applying makeup, and I ran into the garage and hopped on my five-speed bike. Ahhh, I really missed it. As the wind rushed through my long curls, I felt a new sense of purpose. Although Kelly had a new attitude, I knew who she was underneath, and so did Lydia, and we both knew that kissing Eben would ultimately hurt her more than we could bear.

I couldn't stomach the idea of Eben kissing Kelly only to diss her because she had once been overweight. If we didn't try and do something, we would regret it, and I didn't want that. So I decided that Lydia and I needed to save Kelly from kissing Eben. The only way to do that would be to crash the kissing party, which was tonight.

I rode as fast as I could to Lydia's house, so fast that when I arrived I could barely breathe. I waited on her front step until my breathing leveled out, and then I rang her bell. It took a minute, but she opened the door, totally surprised to see me.

"Stacy. What are you doing here?"

"I wanted to say I was sorry. I know it was a bad idea to crash the bar mitzvah. And I'm sorry, but jealousy led me to do it."

We were silent for a minute.

"Well, it was just really embarrassing, and now everyone hates us," Lydia responded.

"I know. I was embarrassed, also. I still am, but I don't care so much if everyone hates us. I just care that Kelly doesn't hate us and that you don't hate me. I just want to be a good friend.

"Will you please accept my apology?" I asked.

"Okay. And I'm sorry I blamed you for everything."

"That's okay," I said. "I'm sorry that you felt embarrassed."

Neither of us knew what to say next. I shrugged and asked, "Friends again?"

"Totally," she said, and we hugged.

Lydia backed up for a second and assessed the scene. "Stacy," Lydia began. "Why are you riding your bike? You know that no one is riding their bike anymore. And your hair. Why isn't your hair straight? And what are you wearing?"

"I don't want to wear their look anymore. I want to wear my look. I want to be comfortable. Now, I'm comfortable. Then? Not so comfortable. Besides, do you know how long it takes to straighten this hair?" I said as I held a sheaf of my heavy brown curls in my hand.

Lydia laughed. "So, I don't get it. We're going back to being ourselves? Who we were before Laila Wertheimer?"

"Yeah. Why not? If The Chicas won't accept us even when we dress and act like them, then what's the point? I felt like I was on *Little House on the Prairie* in those clothes, anyway. We might as well just be who we really are."

Lydia sighed a huge breath of relief.

"Thank God, because I have to tell you something."

"What?" I asked, curious.

"Well . . . follow me." Lydia led me into her living room. "Sit." She commanded. I sat on the couch, and she turned around and opened the bureau drawer and pulled out a long, thick blue ribbon that was attached to a stick. A second later, she held two beautiful peacock-inspired paper fans. Then she pressed PLAY on the nearby stereo and a flute began to play a strange, soft, lilting Asian song. Lydia began to wave the ribbon around, twirling and moving her wrist in a pattern that released the ribbon into a swirl of huge arcs and curved Zs. Then she picked up a fan, raised it in one arm, and twirled, her head bent backward like a figure skater.

"What is this?"

"Chinese ribbon dancing," she said, excited. "Isn't it cool?"

"Well . . . yeah. I mean I've never seen anything like it."

"I saw it on the Olympics and kinda got obsessed with it. I've been taking lessons in secret. But now, since we're not worrying so much about fitting in with The Chicas, I can bring my ribbon dancing out in the open."

I giggled. She was too weird. In the absolute best sense.

She put the ribbon and the fans back in the bureau, and on the way upstairs I told her all about Eben and how disgusting he was about Kelly to his friends. I told her exactly what he said about her weight and that I thought we should go over to the kissing party tonight and prevent Kelly from having her first kiss with this guy. Lydia was adamantly against this.

Lydia stopped on the stairs. "Oh, no. Not again," she said, turning to face me.

"Listen to me—he was saying the worst things about her.

He's going to dump her tomorrow after he kisses her tonight, just because she used to be overweight! This isn't about fitting in anymore, this is about doing the right thing. We are party crashers in the name of rescue, not in the name of self-serving popularity seeking."

Lydia screwed up her face in thought.

"Not in disguise?"

"Nope. As is," I answered.

"And just to help Kelly, not to be part of The Chicas?"

"Exactly. My hands are washed of The Chicas. They don't want me; I don't want them."

Then, without another word, Lydia continued up the stairs and into her closet where she pulled on some jeans, a T-shirt, and her old favorite broken-in ballet slipper shoes.

"Let's hit it."

She got her bike from her garage, and off we went to save our second best friend from one of the worst mistakes of her young adult life.

25. The Kissing Crashers

We could hear people splashing around in the heated pool in the back. We weren't sure whether we should use the front door and walk right into the party, or whether that was breaking and entering. Considering Kelly's home was like our second home, this was a conundrum like no other.

I put my hand on the brass doorknob and let us in to Kelly's house. We could hear people laughing and talking in the kitchen. Lydia and I had planned to waltz through the party and right up to Kelly in order to tell her what we knew. But the minute we were inside, it seemed like it wasn't going to be that easy.

"OH. MY. GOD. If it isn't the little crashers," Eben announced when he saw us. Everyone in the kitchen stopped talking and turned around to stare at us.

"Well, if this isn't the saddest thing I've ever seen. I don't know what is. Oh, wait, yes I do, when you crashed a bar mitzvah!" Kym said. Everyone laughed as she held center court with her Diet Coke. Megan, Sara, Eben, Kelly, and Oliver were standing in a semicircle around her. Eben had his arm around Kelly. Oliver had his arm in the exact same pose around Kym, but when he saw me, he pulled his arm back, alarmed by my presence.

"Beat it, freaks. We don't want what you're selling," Kym said.

"We're here for Kelly, not you," I said.

Kelly met my eye for a brief second.

"Yeah? Well, Kelly told everyone here that she wanted nothing to do with you, that she doesn't even know what she saw in you two to begin with. She never liked you," Kym scolded.

My mouth dropped open, and I turned to Kelly, about to ask her if that was true, when she responded, "Hey, I never said that!" And then stormed out of the room.

"Whatever," Kym said, shrugging her off.

Oliver refilled his glass with Coke, and as soon as he set it down, Eben picked it up, appropriating it as his own. Oliver rolled his eyes.

"You guys are so sad. First you crash my bar mitzvah, and now you crash our party? You're just a couple of crashaholics," Eben said as he drew his arm across his mouth, wiping the Coke from his lip. He turned to Oliver. "See, what did I tell you? My cousin is way cooler than Stacy. She's also not a cheater." And he strutted out of the room.

"I didn't cheat! You know nothing about me!" I called after him.

"We should go after Kelly, don't you think?" Megan asked Sara.

"Probably," Megan responded.

"Listen up, you guys. I have an idea!" Kym crowed while the two girls seemed to roll their eyes in their heads. "Let's go find Kelly. Stat," Kym directed.

Lydia, bless her heart, snuck out of the room and into the den to give Oliver and me a little privacy. He got a new glass, poured more Coke into it, grabbed a nearby straw, and stirred it around. The house was spookily quiet.

"Hi," I said.

"Hi," he replied unenthusiastically.

We were quiet for a little bit. I didn't really know what to say, I just knew that I really, really liked this guy, and if I could unblow what I'd already blown, things might start looking up for me.

"Lydia and I crashed the bar mitzvah because we were jealous that we were the only ones not invited. We wanted to prove we were cool, so we crashed. It was dumb and embarrassing and I wish we hadn't done it, but tonight is different because we heard that Kelly was supposed to kiss Eben for the first time, and I know you're friends with him, but personally I think he's a horrible person and treats people badly, and Kelly deserves to be with someone waaaaay better. So even though we're not really friends anymore, Lydia and I came to save her."

Oliver stood up straighter and turned more in my direction. I wanted him to speak, to accept my apology or say something positive or optimistic, but just as he opened his mouth, Kym and Eben loudly pranced back into the kitchen.

"What are you doing, Oliver?" Eben asked.

"Just talking to Stacy," he answered.

"Well, stop. We need you outside," Eben said. Oliver hung back for a minute, not following, but then Eben turned around and added, "I set this whole thing up, man. You owe me. Don't blow it by standing in here talking to some loser. If you want to practice moving your lips, you will, with my cousin, remember? Now, get outside," Eben demanded, and then Oliver reluctantly followed the two of them. He turned back to me, and I thought I caught a glimpse of apprehension.

26. Love Saves the Day

I went into the den to get Lydia, who was standing at the window with her hand over her eyes, peering out at the girls in the backyard.

"They're getting ready to start making out," she said. "They're pinching their cheeks and fluffing up their hair."

I grabbed her hand. "Let's find Kelly and get out of here."

Outside, girls were bending over and flipping their hair back, applying lip gloss and smoothing out clothing wrinkles. Kelly wasn't among them. Where was she? I started to tell Lydia what had happened with Oliver, but she cut me off suddenly with "Shhh . . . Do you hear that?"

I listened, but all I could hear was the chattering of Kym and The Chicas. Lydia took my hand, and we walked over to the pool house. We opened the screen door and saw Kelly sitting on the couch, with her arms wrapped around her knees, crying. We rushed over to her.

"What's the matter?" Lydia asked.

"Did something happen?" I added.

Kelly shook her head no and then sputtered, "I don't want to make out with Eben!"

"You don't?" I asked, confused.

"No! I don't even like him," she whimpered.

"But you were just saying how great a boyfriend he was, you said it the other day, in homeroom," Lydia said, also confused.

"He bought you a rose," I said, double-checking that she really *didn't* like him.

"No, he didn't. I just said that to impress Kym. I was just . . . playing it all up. I didn't want her to think I was—" and here she stopped.

"A loser?" I asked.

"Yeah," Kelly said.

"Well, we're not losers, either," Lydia said.

"I know. You're not even remotely losers. I just—Kym's just—" And then she started blubbering again, "I don't want to make out with Eben!"

"You don't have to," I said.

"Yes, I do," she sobbed. "Kym and everyone set this whole thing up in order for me to have my first kiss. They even picked the boy, and I don't even like him! I don't know how I'm going to get out of it. They keep telling me I have to."

And then she collapsed into sobs. We put our arms around her.

"We know how to get you out of it," I said.

Kelly looked up, hopeful. "You do?"

"Yup." I nodded.

Kelly was skeptical. "How?"

"Well," I began. "I have an idea."

"Wait—why are you guys being so nice to me?"

Lydia and I looked at each other.

"Because we love you," I said.

"But I've been so mean," she said.

We were all quiet for a minute, not sure exactly how to absorb this.

"Yes. You have," Lydia said, crossing her arms, defensively.

Kelly sniffled, wiped her eyes, and blew her nose. "I tried hard to be friends with both groups, but I was starting to feel like the third wheel with you guys. Ever since you came back from camp, I've felt it even more. The first thing out of your mouths at First Night was about your new fabulous friend you made without me. Laila—" Kelly said with disdainful emphasis. "And then you had planned this big trip to Italy to visit Dante and invited Lydia but not me. I felt, like, totally unnecessary."

"Kelly!" I chided. "You're totally necessary. And besides, all the stuff about Italy was made up."

"It was?" Kelly asked. "Why?"

"Well, first because Dante and I broke up. It happened this summer, and I didn't want to tell you at First Night, but then, everything sort of spun out of control. And besides, you and The Chicas had all these inside jokes that made me jealous, so I guess I wanted you guys to feel left out the way I did."

"You felt jealous?"

"Very!" Lydia said. "You totally dissed us for The Chicas."

"I know, I know. I didn't mean to. Kym is very . . . pressure-y. She's very hard to say no to, she's like Paris Hilton or something. I'm so sorry, you guys. I didn't know what to do. There were just so many different demands being made on me, and I was just convinced that you guys didn't need me anymore. That you were fine on your own and didn't even think of me when I wasn't around."

"Impossible!"

"Never happened!"

"I really am sorry. I don't even really like The Chicas. I mean they should just call themselves The Kyms because Megan and Sara do *everything* Kym tells them to do. It's like they're operating on a community brain. And I'm sorry about Dante, Stacy," Kelly said.

"That's okay. I'm over it. But thanks."

"Well, what are we supposed to do now? All these people are at my house, and I don't even like them!" Kelly said.

"That's where I come in," I said. "And hopefully, Oliver. Who, by the way, better not follow through on kissing Kym tonight, because . . . well, I totally love him."

27. The Cousin of All Surprises!

The Chicas were setting up in the living room. They hadn't even bothered to wait for Kelly, the hostess, before taking the scratchy pillows off the oriental-style couches and setting them down on the floor. How rude.

"First it's Seven Minutes in Heaven, and then we'll play Truth or Dare!" Eben announced to the small throng and winked at Kelly, who cringed.

Lydia, Kelly, and I stood in the doorframe, next to the Persian rug that hung on the wall. Oliver was on the other side of the room and Kym, Megan, and Sara were preening in front of the gilded-framed living-room mirror, applying lip gloss and pulling at their hair with their hands in an attempt to make it straighter. The other kids were pushing the clothes out of the way in the closet.

Kelly snuck around the corner and hid. I went over to Oliver and whispered in his ear. He grabbed the bandanna blindfold off the coffee table, tapped Eben on the shoulder, whispered to him, and then blindfolded him before leading him to the closet. Then he went around the corner to hide.

I tapped Kym on the shoulder.

"What is it, weirdo?" Kym asked me.

"You won. Oliver wants to kiss you, not me. He's waiting for you in the closet, but you have to wear the blindfold." Kym gave me a fake pout and said in a very blasé voice, "Um, hello? Obviously!" I cringed and took the other bandanna off the table and tied it around Kym's eyes. I slowly led Kym to the closet, opened the door, and positioned her in front of Eben.

"Wait until you hear me say 'go,' because you can't start until the door is shut," I told them as I shut the door, almost the entire way.

"Okay, everyone. The first Seven Minutes in Heaven is about to start," I said.

Megan, Sara, and some girls and guys from Eben's school clambered around, standing outside the door. I stood where the crack in the door was so I could see everything.

"Okay, the door is closed," I yelled to them.

Eben put his hands on Kym's shoulders and Kym had her hands on Eben's waist. They just stood there for a minute, breathing in each other's faces, and I heard Kym swallow hard, the way people do when they're nervous. Eben quickly licked his lips like he had the tongue of a dog and very slowly, they leaned in to kiss each other. I opened the door slowly, exposing them to everyone a second before they became official kissing cousins!

They heard the gasps and the giggling and quickly pulled back. Kym whipped off her bandanna and glared at me and Lydia. Eben took his off, and then he gasped. Kym turned and saw that it wasn't Oliver she had kissed, and she gasped.

"Who's the weirdo now?" I asked. Everyone laughed and clapped.

"Ew . . . you were going to kiss your own cousin," Sara yelled.

"Nasty!" Megan called out.

"Wait, no! I didn't know," Kym tried to defend herself. "It was a trick! I was framed!"

Oliver and Kelly rounded the corner. Kym looked at Oliver and Kelly.

"You guys! Save me. You'll never guess what these people did to me."

"We already know. We set it up," Kelly said.

"You? But . . . I thought we were friends."

"Friends don't make other friends do things they don't want to do," Kelly said.

Kym stormed out of the closet. When she got to the front hallway, she turned around and summoned Megan and Sara.

"C'mon, Chicas, move it!" Kym demanded, but they didn't move.

"Kelly's right," Megan said. "You're really bossy."

"Yeah, and not very nice," Sara added.

"WHAT? Are you guys on crack? Get your stuff and let's get out of here!" Kym yelled.

But they didn't budge.

"I can't believe this," Kym said, genuinely shocked by this *coup d'état.* "Eben?" Kym called.

"Yes?" Eben squeaked from the closet.

"C'mon, let's go."

Eben ran out of the closet, grabbed his backpack, and on his way out, grabbed Oliver's arm and dragged him along. Oliver resisted, pulling his arm out of Eben's grip, and said, "Stop trying to control me. I'm not your manservant!"

"Oh, get over yourself, Oliver. If you don't come with me, I'll tell everyone your big secret."

"You almost kissed your cousin. What do I care that I've never kissed anyone before? If that's such a tragic secret, then I don't know what to call *that,*" Oliver said motioning toward the closet with his chin.

Eben was furious but said nothing. Instead, he and Kym hightailed it out of Kelly's house faster than he had pulled away from his cousin's puckered lips. It was a glorious moment, and one I don't think I'll ever forget. Everyone left soon after that, leaving just me, Oliver, Kelly, and Lydia.

"Well, I guess I should go too," Oliver said.

"Okay, thanks for coming over," Kelly said.

"Yeah, it was nice to see you again," Lydia said.

"Will you walk me to the door?" Oliver asked me.

"Sure!" I answered, a little too excitedly.

We stood there for a minute, not doing or saying much of anything.

"Remember those comedy clubs I wanted to go to?" he asked.

"Yeah, I remember."

"Well, they're still just a car ride away. I'd still like to go, if you would."

"I'd love to!" I said.

"And while we're there, we can look up my old friend who lives on Fifth-seventh Street—Winnie Foster."

I blushed and playfully smacked his arm. "Stop it," I flirted.

"Couldn't resist. So it's a date. I'll call you."

"Okay, great."

"It was nice to meet you, Stacy Friedman."

"It was nice to meet you, too, Oliver Solomon."

And then, he leaned down, and I smelled his Coca-Cola and pretzel breath. And then I felt his very soft lips as they met mine and we kissed, right then and there, on Kelly's front step for, like, a full minute. Then he turned around and slowly walked away, while I held on to the side of the door and tried not to faint.

When I walked back into the house, Kelly's and Lydia's heads were sticking out from behind the wall, spying on us.

"Did he stick his tongue in your mouth?" Lydia asked.

"Stop it, stop it, stop it!" Kelly squealed, already disgusted.

Lydia didn't budge.

"Well, did he?" she asked, leaning forward waiting for the answer. She studied me intently, wouldn't take her eyes off me, and then Kelly and I both fell over laughing. We stayed up almost the entire night giggling, gossiping, and catching up. Most important, we made a pact. We were going to remain true to ourselves, no matter the cost.

"Hey, guys," I said, before we all fell asleep. "If a mute swears, does his mother wash his hands with soap?"

28. The End of Winniver—
The Start of Staciver

The next day at my house, Lydia, Kelly, my mother, Alan, and I sat in chairs, in a row, in Arthur's bedroom. We were all awaiting the unveiling and presentation of the room-cleaning robot. Eliza came out first. "Ladies and gentlemen, thank you for coming to the Arthur Lab. Today's unveiling was brought to you by—" Eliza turned to Arthur, who had been mouthing along like he was a stage mother. Eliza looked lost, desperate. She had forgotten her lines.

"Come here," Arthur whispered to her. Eliza walked over to Arthur, and he whispered in her ear. They both giggled, and then Eliza came back to the "stage."

"Today's unveiling has been brought to you by The Friedman Foundation of Overachieving Children."

Eliza ran off the stage and joined Arthur. Together, they opened his closet, and there, gleaming silver, was Oman Hudi. Arthur clapped twice, and Oman Hudi rolled forward. Arthur looked at Eliza, and she clapped twice, and Oman rolled backward. Then Arthur plugged something in; Eliza stood in front of Oman and dropped some coffee grounds onto the carpet (at which point my mother gasped). Then Arthur clapped twice, and Oman Hudi became very loud as he rolled forward over the coffee grounds. When Oman Hudi reached the other side, the coffee grounds had disappeared.

My mother's jaw was dropped. Alan was shaking his head, side to side, the motion saying *Unbelievable*. Lydia and Kelly were standing, craning their necks trying to witness an actual shopping cart with a tinfoiled head vacuum Arthur's bedroom. It was pretty damn impressive. So impressive that we all started clapping, giving Arthur his due. But Oman Hudi responded to our clapping and started to roll backward and forward, vacuuming the same spot over and over and faster and faster as we continued to applaud, until some clicking noises started to rise from inside him.

"STOP IT! STOP IT!" Arthur yelled. "YOU'RE KILLING HIM!"

Everyone froze midclap as the robot started to smoke.

"Hmm. We'll have to do something about that," Eliza said. "Maybe implant a less sensitive microphone?"

Arthur nodded and reached for his tools. "Great idea."

* * *

Later that afternoon, Megan and Sara and, yes, Marni Gross, came over for a while and the five of us went swimming. Inviting Marni seemed like the right thing to do, especially after everything that happened to Lydia and me. While we were wrapping ourselves in towels so we could hang out on the lounge chairs in the sun, we saw a lone figure in a bright red top walking toward us. Megan sat up. "Hey, is that Kym?"

We all sat up and stared. Sure enough, Kym Armstrong was walking toward us. When she reached us, we all stared at one another. I still felt a twinge of fear, but not as much as I would have a couple days earlier.

"I'm sorry I was mean," Kym announced.

Which one of us was she talking to? We all looked up at her, confused. None of us responded.

"I'm talking to all of you. I was mean to all of you, and I apologize. My mom made me come and tell you."

I rolled my eyes.

"Well, that was thoughtful of her."

"So, can I like, hang out with you guys? I brought my own towel and everything."

"On one condition," Kelly said.

"What?" Kym asked.

"That you realize there is no leader here. We're all

friends. No one is more important than the other."

Kym seemed to think about this for a second.

"Well, I can't make any promises. But I'll try."

"Trying is good," Marni said.

"Yeah, but we need a promise," Lydia said.

Kym crossed her arms and appeared ready to stomp her feet in tantrum mode. And then, in a voice I can only say sounded like mine when I was yelling at my mother, Kym rolled her eyes, tossed her head back with annoyed defeat, and said, "Fine. God. Okay. I'll do it."

Then she spread out her towel and lay down on a chaise.

After the girls left, I spent about an hour making beds and cleaning the house (I had to earn back the bat mitzvah money I spent—in labor). Just as all the hospital corners were made and all the lint had been vacuumed, the doorbell rang. I ran downstairs and answered the door to Oliver Solomon. His mother waited in the car.

"You ready?" he asked.

"Ready and steady," I said. "Bye, Mom!" I screamed up the stairs.

She hung her head over the bannister and looked down.

"Have fun, you two. And thank you to your mother, Oliver."

"Okay, Mrs. Friedman," Oliver said, and then he opened the door and out we went, into Mrs. Solomon's car, toward New York City to go to Caroline's. Our first ever comedy show.

In the car on the way into the city, I asked Oliver and his mom a very pressing question. "If you jog backward, will you gain weight?"

They both laughed, and Oliver and I leaned back into the seat. He turned to me and said, "I poured spot remover on my dog. Now he's gone."

"I used to have an open mind but my brain kept falling out," I said.

"What happens if you get scared half to death, twice?" Oliver offered.

"Where there's a will, I want to be in it!"

Oliver pretended to tap a microphone, and I said, "Is this thing on?"

And Oliver took the pretend microphone from me and said into it, "That's all folks, we'll be here all week!" Then he handed me back the fake mike and squeezed my hand.

29. Back at the Cool Table

Well, God, I will not deny that so far, eighth grade has been tumultuous. A drama for a sitcom lover is not appreciated. But I suppose, even God needs entertainment. Next time, though, just send money. Kidding.

I really thought that Laila Wertheimer knew it all, that clothes make the person. But I guess she was wrong, because I'm not dressed as anyone other than myself, and I'm starting to feel pretty darn good.

I wanted to thank you for helping me and Lydia to get Kelly back. It turns out, while we don't know exactly who we are yet, we both know one thing: we're excellent at being good friends. And even though it got really tough at times, it was worth everything along the way.

Oh, and God? Thanks for Oliver! He is the cutest, most best boyfriend in the world. We went to Caroline's yesterday, and this weekend we're going to an all-ages *open mike at the mall. But you want to know the best part about it? He just gets me, and all my jokes too.*

Love,

Stacy Adelaide Friedman

P.S. A blonde girl enters a store that sells curtains. She tells the salesman, "I would like to buy a pink curtain the size of my computer screen." The surprised salesman replies, "But, madam, computers do not wear curtains!" . . . And the blonde says, "Helloooo . . . ? I've got Windows. . . ." Ba-dum-dum.

Acknowledgments

As always, thanks go to my very supportive friends and family who helped usher me through deadlines and forgave my delayed responses to calls and e-mails. I would especially like to thank my editor, Siobhan Vivian, for her extensive and insanely skilled edits, and Josh Bank, Ben Schrank, and Leslie Morgenstein for welcoming me aboard the good ship Alloy. Thanks also to Alessandra Balzer and all the kind and understanding folks at Hyperion. To Judy Goldschmidt for the initial introduction and hand holding; and the NYC middle-school kids at Calhoun, Nightingale Bamford, Little Red School House, P.S. 286, Albert Leonard Middle School, and the kids at the JCC in Phoenix, Arizona, for sharing their hilarious rite-of-passage horror stories with me. Also thanks to Donna Brodie and the Writers' Room. Finally, thanks go to Andrew Blauner for his love, loyalty, and support along the way.